STORM SURGE

KERRI LEWIS

DEDICATION

This book is dedicated to my marvelous mother, Joanne Taylor, my first reader and greatest fan. I would also like to thank my friends who previewed the book and gave me critiques and insights, especially, Carl, Kathi and Susan. You all made me a better writer.

PROLOGUE

Phirun Neak locked the door to his restaurant and carried the take-out bag with dinner for his family to his car. It was 9:00 p.m. A little late for dinner, but this had been their tradition for years, first just for him and his wife, and then all four of them once the girls got older. Tonight, there would just be three of them since his oldest daughter was away at college.

He beamed with pride as he thought of his eldest child. She was the first in the family to go to college; and not just any college, but Stanford, on a scholarship. She was a smart girl, and she worked very hard. He knew she would do well. He had worked hard these past twenty-five years after fleeing Cambodia for just this reason.

Phirun pulled into his driveway and parked the car. He handed two take-out boxes to his wife, Bopha, as he kissed her on the cheek. She would put the dinner out on the table. He took the other two take-out boxes to his den.

Although he practiced most of the customs of his adopted country, he was still leery of putting all his money in the bank. He knew too well how governments could be toppled and assets lost overnight. He did have a bank account; over the years he had learned that other businesses and the government preferred to deal with checks, not cash. But he only put in the amount necessary to just cover those expenses. The rest he kept hidden in various places in the house.

Phirun took the cash from that day's business out of the other two take-out boxes and laid it on his desk. He counted and recorded the amount in his ledger. He quickly calculated the percentage that was profit and put that amount back into one of the boxes. The rest he put in a bank deposit bag to take to the bank on the way to work in the morning.

On the way to the dining room, Phirun stashed the box with the cash in the kitchen pantry. He joined his wife and daughter at the table, where they dined on vegetable spring rolls and stir-fry eggplant with coconut pork. They were both specialties of his restaurant.

A knock on the door interrupted their dinner. Their daughter rose to answer it. The Neaks had learned over the years that, as in most American households, phone calls and visitors at nighttime were usually for the teenagers. Phirun watched his daughter as she walked toward the front door. Dara was blossoming into a lovely young woman. She was also a good student. In a few years, she would join her sister at college. He was a fortunate man.

When Dara opened the door, two men wearing black ski masks burst through the door. One of them grabbed Dara and held a knife to her throat. Phirun sprang to his feet. Bopha screamed. The man who was not holding Dara closed and locked the door. He was the taller of the two men and it soon became apparent that he was the leader. He turned and approached Dara's parents.

"Sit down and shut up," he ordered them, and then he motioned to his shorter, muscular accomplice to bring the girl over. He shoved her in her chair and continued to address the family. "Sorry to interrupt your dinner, please, continue eating."

The shorter man stood behind Dara, holding the knife at her back while the leader walked around the adjoining living and dining rooms, casually observing their belongings. He stopped when he came to a family picture. He picked it up and looked at it more closely. "Nice family," he said. "Where is your other daughter tonight?"

The Neaks did not answer. He walked back over to the table, put the picture down, and sat in the empty fourth chair. "I asked you where your other daughter was." He nodded at the man behind Dara, who grabbed Dara's hair and pulled her head back sharply.

"She's at college," Phirun blurted out.

"College? Where?"

"California."

"I like California. I go there sometimes. Which college? Berkeley, U.C.L.A, Stanford?" The taller masked man observed the husband and wife exchange a quick glance when he mentioned Stanford. "Stanford, huh. So, she's a smart girl. Let's hope her parents are too."

He reached over and grabbed Bopha's plate and started eating. "This is good. Take out from your restaurant, isn't it? In fact, it's so good, I want some more. Did you bring any more boxes home with you, Mr. Neak," he asked looking directly into Phirun's eyes.

"No, this is all the food I brought home."

The lead man rose from his chair and slowly strode over to Phirun and slapped him across the face. Then he calmly bent down until he was eye level with Phirun and said, "You're not listening. I didn't ask you if you had any more fucking food, I asked you if you brought any more take-out boxes home with you tonight."

Phirun silently cursed himself. They knew, he thought, they knew about the money. He had gotten careless recently; always putting the money in take-out boxes, leaving at the same time every night, too many boxes for three people for food. They must have been watching him, figured it out. He tried to size up the masked men.

Even with their masks, Phirun could tell that they were Asian. He knew they must be with a gang. Phirun knew he had to be careful. He had some experience with Asian gangs in California.

One evening, a few months after he opened his first restaurant in Long Beach, some Asian teenage gang members burst into his place. They shoved him against the counter and held him there while they smashed some chairs and broke out the front window. They demanded all the money that he had in the cash register and told him that he had to pay them some money every week if he didn't want this to happen again.

Phirun had been furious. He came to America to get away from corruption and the threat of violence. He reported it to the police, but they did nothing about it. The next week the gang returned and beat him to a pulp, saying they didn't want to see a police car outside his restaurant ever again. He paid them their weekly fee after that and had no more problems, except in his head.

He resented being victimized by his own people. This was America, and he was not going to put up with it. He and Bopha worked even harder, saving most of what they made, studying every spare minute until they passed the citizenship test. When Bopha got pregnant, he knew it was time to move on. He sold his business, took his savings and moved the family to Oklahoma.

He specifically chose not to live or work in Little Saigon in Oklahoma City. He heard it was safe, but he didn't want to take any chance of living under the jurisdiction of another Asian gang. Besides, they were Americans now and would live in the general population. He thought Bethany was a friendly place and found a good location for another restaurant.

Phirun's mind raced as he quickly tried to gauge the gravity of the situation. He had heard that gang activity had been picking up in Oklahoma City. But they had never ventured into the suburbs before. Could these just be some rogue punks out for some quick cash? How much did they know? Did they know he kept money hidden in the house? Probably not. If they had been watching him then they knew that he made a drop at the bank every morning. He would give them the bank deposit bag on his desk. That's what they came for.

"I apologize. I misunderstood," Phirun answered the man. "I brought some money home in another box to count and take to the bank tomorrow morning. It's in a bank bag now, on my desk, in my den. You can take it. Please do not hurt my family."

"That's better," the lead masked man said as he walked back

around the table and sat back down. He pulled out a gun and pointed it at Bopha. He spoke in Vietnamese to the other man, telling him to go and find the bag and find something to tie them up with. The other man released his grip on Dara and left the room. Then he turned to Bopha and addressed her in English.

"So, what other valuables do you have in the house? Any jewelry?"

Bopha looked over at her husband nervously. He nodded at her and told her to give the man her rings. Tears rolled down her face as she slipped them off her fingers and slid them across the table.

The shorter, stockier robber returned with the deposit bag, some rope and a few take-out boxes. He dropped the bag and boxes on the table. "I found them in a cupboard when looking for rope," he told the lead man. Then he started tying the women to their chairs.

The lead man opened the take-out boxes. Phirun's face turned ashen. The lead man calmly closed the boxes and looked at Phirun. "You love your family, don't you," he asked Phirun coolly. He stood up without waiting for an answer, walked over to Bopha, who was tied into her chair, and kicked the chair over backwards to the floor. She landed with a crack and screamed in pain. "Then why do you make me hurt them," he continued.

Phirun jumped up from his chair but the other man tackled him in an instant. He held him on the floor where he could see his wife, as the lead man took a switchblade out of his boot and flicked it open. Bopha was lying still in the chair with her back on the floor, whimpering. The lead robber ripped open her shirt and cut off her bra.

"No," Phirun screamed. "Don't." The lead man nodded to his partner, who immediately administered a forceful blow to Phirun's gut.

"Don't fucking interrupt me." He bent down and cut a small heart shape on the top of her left breast. "What do you love more, Mr. Neak, your wife or," he paused and moved the blade down her chest and deftly carved a large dollar sign across her abdomen. "Money."

Phirun watched in horror as Bopha cried out in pain and blood started trickling down her belly. "My wife, my wife," Phirun cried out. "Please stop. You can take all my money."

The lead man stood up and wiped the blood off the blade with the table cloth. "Wise choice. Now get up." The other man released Phirun and he stood up. Without any warning, the lead man unleashed a torrent of kicks and body blows on Phirun. In minutes, Phirun was back on the floor. "Didn't you hear me? I said get your ass up and take me to collect all the money you have stashed in the house. Oh, and if I was you, I'd hurry, because my friend here keeps eyeing your daughter and he is not a patient man."

Phirun could not disguise the anguish he felt as he watched the other man pull his daughter's chair away from the table and start to unbutton her blouse. Bopha's whimpering now turned into a wail. "Go," she yelled at her husband in Khmer, "Go quickly and give them all the money."

Phirun rushed through the house gathering all the money he had hidden inside. It was his life savings, but it didn't matter any longer. The lead man trailed behind him with a large trash bag that he had Phirun place the money in as they uncovered each hidden cache.

When they returned, Dara's breasts were exposed, and her jeans and panties were around her ankles. The other man was laughing as he groped her everywhere he could reach. Dara was crying and trying to free herself from the chair and the man's hands.

"Stop! Stop! I gave you all the money, I swear," Phirun yelled as he ran into the room. "Stop! Please, I have done as you asked."

The lead man shoved him into a chair and held a gun to his head. "Shut up. I give the orders. We have one more matter to settle before we leave." He nodded to the other man who untied Dara and threw her on the floor. He held her down with one hand and his body weight while he used the other hand to unzip his pants.

"Please, please I'm begging you, don't hurt my daughter," Phirun pleaded. Tears streamed down his face.

The lead man looked at Phirun callously and said, "No police, no doctors or we'll come back here and then pay a little visit to California. I like college girls."

"Yes, yes, I promise. No police, no doctors. Please make him stop."

"Okay," the lead man called over his shoulder to his partner. "Let's go." Then he cracked Phirun over the head with the butt of his gun. Phirun crumpled to the floor. He grabbed the bag and turned to leave, expecting to hear the other man right behind him. But instead he heard a rhythmic thumping sound. Dara started sobbing. The tall man looked down at the floor.

"Chien, that's enough," he shouted. But it was too late. Chien was on the verge of coming and John Nguyen knew he couldn't get him to stop now. It was supposed to be just the threat of rape, but sometimes Chien went too far. Oh well, it might be an even better deterrent this way; they still have another daughter.

John Nguyen and Chien left the house with a large trash bag full of cash, knowing that this crime would never be reported. And John Nguyen thought, with all the loot they took, Uncle Bao would agree that expanding the Pham organization's reach to the suburbs was a smart move. It would be another feather in his cap. He would be Uncle Bao's first lieutenant in no time. He would have to remember to thank Stuart for the tip on this Neak character.

CHAPTER 1

As Janet Reed stood peering over the edge of the cliff near the lighthouse, the cold Pacific wind pierced her breastbone and whistled through the cavernous space where her heart used to be. The thunderous crack of the waves against the rocks below and the barely audible whoosh of the water being sucked back out to sea mesmerized her. She was seduced by the rhythm of the ocean and oddly comforted by its crushing force. She imagined she was the wave, one moment powerful, the next powerless. Powerful, powerless, powerful, powerless, over and over again for eternity. One step, it would be so easy.

"There's a bench over here if you would like to sit down and watch the ocean," a voice called out from behind her. Janet snapped out of her trance. She had no idea how long she had been standing there, but now became aware that she was shaking. Slowly, Janet backed up and sat down on the bench behind her without looking at the man sitting there.

To avoid conversation, Janet turned and surveyed the lighthouse that sat near the edge of the cliff. A tower of cold white stone rose up from the ground. There were no windows in the tower, only cracks and crevices formed by years of standing sentinel in the cruel Pacific wind. A smaller, wood planked structure resembling a turret topped the stone tower. Dark, lifeless windows dotted the wooden structure. A computer now ran the beacon light that sat inside the turret. There was no need for the watchful eye of a keeper.

A weathered bronze dome with a seagull statue perched on top covered the beacon room. Janet looked up at the statue and shivered as another gust of wind blew in from the ocean. She felt sorry for the poor bird, sitting there, frozen in time, trying to draw its wings into its body, exposed and alone.

The man finally spoke again. "The rugged beauty of the ocean is captivating isn't it?" he said. "I stop here everyday on my walks. It's rare that I find another soul up here anymore. Is this your first time here?"

"Yes" Janet said, finding her voice.

"Are you new to town or just visiting?"

"Visiting for a few weeks."

Janet looked up at the man. His eyes met hers. They were strong, youthful eyes, although the wrinkles, or lifelines, as her grandmother used to call them, betrayed his life experience. Still, he looked pretty fit for a man who she guessed must be in his late 50's. He reached over and shook her hand.

"Jonathon Briggs" he said, "I live in the house up the cliff, behind the lighthouse."

"Janet Reed"

"Well Miss Reed, I suppose I will share my favorite spot with you since you are only here for a few weeks, but don't tell anyone else about it. The feeling of isolation is part of the charm of this place."

"That works for me."

They both turned forward and watched the seagulls hovering over the lighthouse, riding the thermal air currents. Janet took a few deep breaths, relaxed her shoulders and let her arms fall to the bench. Her left hand came to rest on a plaque. She turned to read it.

"Break! Break! Break!

On the cold gray stones, O sea!

9

And I would that my tongue could utter

The thoughts that arise in me.

-Tennyson

Dedicated to the memory of Sarah Monroe"

"What a profound poem for this spot," Janet said. "Who was Sarah Monroe?"

"She was a local teenager who died last spring. She liked to watch the ocean from this cliff."

Janet felt an instant affinity with the girl and wanted to know more. "Did you know her?"

"Not well. She started coming up here last winter for hours at a time. She was always writing in a book or deep in thought. We would speak occasionally. A few months after she died, the church group that she belonged to put the bench with the plaque here."

He stood up as he ended his explanation. "Well Ms. Reed, I must continue on my walk. Have a pleasant stay and remember our deal."

"Thank you I will." Janet watched as Jonathon Briggs strolled up the path behind the lighthouse. She decided it was time for her to leave as well and headed down the cliff path toward the beach, purposely avoiding looking back over the edge of the cliff. Robert would be wondering where she was.

She had only gone on this walk to keep Robert from pestering her about spending too much time in the cottage. Why did she even bother to come along on his business trip? He works all the time whether he's at home or away from home.

It was Robert's idea that she come along. "The Bay area is beautiful and cool this time of year. One of my clients is going to let us use his weekend cottage south of San Francisco on the peninsula in San Mateo County. It's right by the ocean with a beautiful vista of the Pacific shoreline. Come on, it'll be a great break from the Texas heat, and we'll be able to spend some more time together. This trip isn't going to be all work you know."

She had pretended to buy Robert's sales pitch and agreed to come along, but she knew the truth. He was afraid to leave her home alone.

Janet cautiously climbed over a large pile of small flat rocks as she made her way up from the beach, back to the cottage. She stopped and picked one up. It felt cool and smooth. She turned it over in her hand again and again. It was just an ordinary grey stone but years of pounding by the Pacific Ocean had turned it into a tactile delight. This would be a great stone for Daniel's rock collection. She slipped the stone into her pocket and continued on her way.

Thinking of Daniel made her smile. She wished her son were there with her now. He had always been fascinated by rocks. Janet and Daniel spent many hours of his childhood hiking the greenbelts of Barton Creek, looking for rocks. When it was warm enough, they would search in the creek as well. Only rocks with some type of unique marking or characteristic made it into his collection. She reached into her pocket and rubbed the stone between her fingers and smiled again. Daniel would be pleased.

When she got back to the cottage, Robert was at the table furiously typing on his laptop. He looked up as she came in.

"I'm trying to finish this proposal for Jack Allen's company. How was your walk?"

"Fine. I found a lovely spot to…."

"Did I mention that we are having dinner with the Allens tonight at The Outrigger? I'm going to pitch my proposal to his board on Saturday so I thought I should grease the wheels a little."

Janet dreaded these dinners but felt strangely upbeat after her discovery at the lighthouse cliff. "Well I guess I'd better go dress for the part. How long do I have to *beautify*?"

"We're meeting them in an hour."

Janet walked toward the door to the bedroom, then suddenly

stopped and turned to Robert. She reached into her pocket.

"Oh, I forgot to tell you. I found a great rock on the beach for Daniel's collection." She placed the rock on the table and went into the bedroom, softly humming.

Robert watched as his wife went into the bedroom. He took off his glasses, closed his eyes and pinched the bridge of his nose. He didn't know what to do with his wife anymore. He sighed, put his glasses back on and went back to his work. Daniel Reed died three months ago.

CHAPTER 2

The Outrigger sits at the edge of Montara Beach State Park, overlooking the ocean. Looking out of its massive three-story windows, Janet felt as if she were floating on the surf. Robert tugged at her elbow.

"There they are," he said as he waved. Jack and Melissa Allen were seated at a table in the far corner that had an ocean view from two sides.

"I snagged the best table in the place for us," Jack said, rising to shake Robert's hand. "And this must be your better half," he continued, taking Janet's hand in his.

Robert put his arm around Janet and said, "Janet, I would like you to meet my favorite clients, Jack and Melissa Allen."

"Nice to meet you," Janet said as she slid into the chair next to Melissa that Robert had pulled out for her. He was always more attentive to her when they were out with clients. It was one of the few benefits of coming along.

"Please call me Missy. How is the cottage?"

"Oh, it is just lovely," Janet replied. "Thank you so much for letting us use it."

"Nothing but the best for the family of the man who is going to make me rich, right Robert," Jack chuckled.

"Well, that's the general idea," Robert said, glancing at Janet out of the corner of his eye. The reference to family seemed fairly innocuous, but he never knew what would set her off. She seemed to be doing better lately, but after that rock incident this afternoon he wasn't so sure.

Missy caught his glance and picked up her menu. "Shall we order? I am starving."

They ordered and sipped on wine while talking about the weather and national news items. It wasn't long before the conversation turned to Robert's merger plan for Jack's company. Robert gently squeezed Janet's hand under the table. This was his signal for Janet to engage the wife in other conversation.

"Excuse me gentlemen, y'all don't mind if I monopolize Missy's time for a few minutes? I have so many questions about the area."

"Oh, go right ahead," Jack said, "Missy is an expert on the area, especially the shops along Main Street in Half Moon Bay."

Janet turned toward Missy.

"Jack's right, I love this area," Missy said. "We've been coming down here most weekends for years. Have you been to Main Street yet? It really is quaint, and the artsy stores are fun to explore."

"I haven't ventured out much. I've just been relaxing at the cottage and the beach. Thank you again. It's such a great place."

"Our pleasure. Say, why don't I come down Saturday, we could have lunch and browse through some of the shops. The guys will be tied up in a meeting all day."

"Sure, that sounds nice." Janet wasn't sure how nice it would really be, but she knew this was part of her duties when she went with Robert on his business trips.

"So," Missy continued, "what are your questions?"

"Well, this may seem rather strange, but I was wondering if you knew of a girl named Sarah Monroe who died this past spring and what church she used to belong to?"

Missy hesitated and picked at the food on her plate. Janet sensed she was uncomfortable. God knows what Robert told her.

"I was up at the old lighthouse this afternoon and sat on a bench that has a plaque on it, with a poem about the ocean," Janet explained. "It was dedicated to a Sarah Monroe. A man who was up there told me it was one of her favorite spots and that the church she belonged to had the plaque installed a few months after she died.

I just thought what a wonderful thing - to put a plaque with a poem at a loved one's favorite spot. Most people in Texas leave crosses and flowers at the spot where they died, not where they lived or liked to be. I wanted to go by and visit with someone at the church to see how they went about getting the plaque and permission from the city to place it on public property. I was thinking it might be a nice thing to do for Daniel."

Missy was surprised at how openly Janet spoke about death and that she mentioned Daniel. Robert had told her that Janet was having a difficult time coping with Daniel's death and that it would be best not to mention it. Feeling ill at ease, Missy decided to focus on the story of Sarah Monroe.

"Well, I didn't know Sarah Monroe personally, but I knew who she was. We go to the church that she belonged to on the weekends that we are in town. It's Trinity Church at the corner of Main and Poplar Street. Sarah was in the youth group there and the youth minister, Paul Barnett, was the driving force behind the lighthouse bench.

The plaque, however, caused a bit of a controversy in the church and the community at first. Pastor Paul and Sarah's mother wanted a scripture verse on the plaque, but since it was on public land, some in the community thought that would be inappropriate. Eventually a compromise was reached. In fact, the man that you said you met up there, did he tell you his name?"

"Yes, Jonathon Briggs."

"I thought so. He was the one who came up with poem that was eventually used, which was funny because originally, he was against the bench being put there in the first place. He's an old English professor who moved here about a year ago. He lives up on the ridge behind the lighthouse, kind of a hermit, really likes his privacy."

"He hinted at that today. But why would he be against the bench?"

"He said he didn't want people to come up there and brood. He had better things to do with his time then be on suicide watch?"

Janet briefly wondered if his arrival at the cliff this afternoon had truly been coincidental, but her interest about Sarah was piqued. "Did she commit suicide? There at the lighthouse?"

"Well, no one seems to know for sure, that's kind of a long story." Missy said, still hesitant to go into details about anyone's death around Janet.

"Well," Janet said, looking over at Robert and Jack with their heads close together in conversation, "it looks like we have time."

Janet grinned at Missy. Their eyes met. Missy reached over and laid her hand on Janet's. "Janet, I'm so…"

"It's okay, thank you," Janet said, gently squeezing Missy's hand, sparing them both the awkward conversation of condolences. "Go on, I want to hear the story."

"Well let's see," Missy began, "Sarah had lived here just six months before her death last March. I remember when they arrived in October, because we were down at the cottage that weekend. Sarah and her mother had just moved into the apartment at the Nursing Home where Charlene, Sarah's mom, had just been hired as the cook.

Betsy Massing, the director of the Cresthaven Nursing Home, is a member of Trinity Church and brought the Monroes with her that Sunday. The Ladies Guild got all excited when they found out the Monroes were from Louisiana. Betsy had already told some of

16

the ladies that the Monroes had arrived with practically nothing.

These women thought they were going to be able give some hands-on help to Hurricane Katrina victims. Of course, the church had already taken up a collection and sent some money to aid organizations in New Orleans, but this was helping victims in the flesh. So, they set about collecting clothes, pantry items and furniture to help setup the Monroes' apartment.

Well, when Charlene heard about it, she would have nothing to do with it. She said she and Sarah were from Shreveport, Louisiana, not New Orleans, and they did not need charity, especially when there were so many real victims of the hurricane that needed the help.

Not to be deterred, the Ladies Guild scaled-back a little on the collections and gave Sarah and Charlene brightly decorated baskets of food, clothes and school supplies and called it a welcome gift from their new church home."

Missy took a sip of wine before she continued. "Charlene and Sarah came to church every Sunday with Betsy. It's all anyone from town saw of them for a while, since Charlene worked six days a week as a cook and Sarah was home schooled. I think I recall Betsy telling me that Sarah also worked part-time as an aide at the home.

Anyway, Pastor Paul started visiting them at the nursing home. The church has an active outreach program. And, after a few visits, Sarah started coming to youth group on Wednesday nights. Charlene came with her at first and then joined one of the Wednesday night Bible study groups."

"That's all very interesting, but I don't see how that relates to her death," Janet interrupted, hoping to refocus Missy's story. Sometimes, Janet's investigative reporting background slipped out, especially when she was impatient. She didn't know how much more time Robert would give her.

"Sorry, I guess I've been rambling. I really know more about her history with the church, than her death. Although, there have been plenty of rumors over the months."

"Such as…"

"Okay, I'll try and piece them together for you. She died last March. Apparently, she went for walk in the late afternoon. Her mother said she liked to walk along the shore and up the cliffs by the lighthouse. When she didn't come home in time to help serve dinner to the residents, Charlene began to worry. According to Betsy, when a rain squall blew in from the Pacific around seven o'clock that evening, she started to get frantic, but she wouldn't let Betsy call the police. Instead, they called Pastor Paul."

"What did he do?"

"I'm told that he searched the shoreline, climbed up on the cliffs and looked around the lighthouse, but he didn't find her. He went back and sat with Charlene the rest of the night. He told her that Sarah was probably visiting with a friend and lost track of time. They made a few calls to some of the other youth group members. Finally, around midnight Pastor Paul convinced Charlene to call the police."

"And did they find her?"

"Not right away. They asked if she had a boyfriend or any reason to run away from home, you know, usual teenage stuff. Charlene insisted that she didn't. The police told her not to worry, that Sarah would probably show up in a few hours, but that they would notify patrols to keep an eye out for her. They assured her that if Sarah hadn't shown up by daybreak, they would mount a full-scale search, including the area Pastor Paul already searched.

She never came home. The police found her the next morning, wedged between two rocks below the lighthouse cliff. Pastor Paul felt horrible that he missed her in his search. The police said it would have been hard to spot anyone down there at night, especially with high waves from the surge caused by the squall. Charlene was devastated."

"That poor girl's mother, what an agonizing night, waiting, not knowing, and then…." Janet closed her eyes and rubbed her temples. Robert looked down at the end of the table and saw his wife.

"Say, would you gals like some dessert?"

"That would be delightful." Missy answered. Janet glanced over at Robert, "Sure, I could use some chocolate."

"Great, I'll get the waiter to bring the dessert cart."

Janet looked back at Missy and tried to make light of her pause. She really did want Missy to continue. "Sorry about that, low blood sugar, I guess. A girl can't go too long without chocolate you know. So anyway, was it suicide?"

"As far as I know, the coroner's report was inconclusive and there was no suicide note. I really don't know the details, but Pastor Paul might. Charlene sort of fell apart for while after Sarah's death and he took it upon himself to look after her and all the burial and investigation details. They both insisted Sarah would never commit suicide and that it must have been a tragic accident.

There was also some commotion about a blue notebook or journal. Several people told police she used to keep one."

"Yes, Mr. Briggs mentioned she was always writing in something when he saw her."

"Actually, he likes to be called Professor Briggs. Anyway, no one could find the notebook. They searched her room, the nursing home, the cliffs and the shoreline, but it never turned up."

"What was so important about the notebook?"

"The police thought that it might give a clue as to what happened or maybe contain a suicide note. Charlene wanted to find it because she wanted to keep Sarah's writings, she didn't have very much else to remember her by, and to prove that it didn't contain a suicide note."

"Ladies," Jack called from the other end of the table, "you have got to see this. I hope you're not on a diet." Janet and Missy turned back toward their husbands and the dessert cart.

CHAPTER 3

Janet was just finishing up her sun salutations on the deck of the cottage, when Robert came out to say goodbye. "Yoga by the sea, huh. I wish I had the discipline to be as fit as you. Sorry I've got to rush off," he said as he bent down to kiss her.

They both drank a little too much wine last night and Robert spent an extra hour in bed this morning. Janet wasn't sure if he was hung over or just avoiding her after last night's fight. They rarely fought. Avoidance was more their style. Yet last night, they both came uncorked.

On the way home from the restaurant, Janet mentioned to Robert that she wanted to research getting a bench with a poem for Daniel.

"Where would we put it?" Robert said as he shifted in his seat, gripping the wheel tighter, trying not to show his agitation, "in his room next to his growing rock collection?"

"What's that supposed to mean?" Janet replied.

"It means you are driving me crazy! One minute you act as if Daniel is still alive and with us and the next you want to erect a monument in his name."

"I didn't say I wanted to *erect* anything!"

"Believe me, you have made that perfectly clear the last few months."

"Oh, so now this is about you. Poor Robert. Not getting any."

"Stop it Janet. Listen to me, Daniel is dead. Nothing you can do will bring him back. You have to let go. Move on."

"Don't you dare tell me what I have to do," Janet screamed, unleashing the frustration and agonizing devastation she had been choking down like castor oil the last few months. "It's so easy for you. You act like he never existed. Just go off to work like you always do, like you always did. I can't do that. Daniel was a part of my life every day, not just when it was convenient for me."

"Convenient for me! Janet that's bullshit and you know it. I loved Daniel as much as you did. All the time I spent away I was working for the family. To make a better life for all of us."

"Oh, like the time you bailed out of our family fun run for a golf game." Robert still felt guilty about missing the fun run, especially since it turned out to be their last family outing. Janet knew that mentioning it up would bring a swift end to the conversation. It worked. They drove the rest of way home in silence.

Janet closed her eyes and thought about the fun run. Robert could not make her give up her memories. They were what validated Daniel's existence and the only thing that still made her smile.

The fun run had been Daniel's idea. At first it was going to be a family activity. Robert, Janet and Daniel could all train together for a month and then run the race. In the end, Robert begged off training because of work obligations but promised to be there to take a picture of Janet and Daniel as they crossed the finish line. "I'll be the support team. All first-class athletes need a support team."

Although they did train, it was sporadic at best, which, Janet realized the day before the race, was fine for a ten-year-old, but not the best course of action if you are trying to run a three-mile race at thirty-seven. To make matters worse, their "support team" had an unexpected client come to town who needed a fourth for his tee time the next morning. "Sorry guys," Robert had explained, "Trust me, with this guy; it's more business than pleasure. I would much rather be at the finish line with you, but unfortunately, duty calls." Once again, Janet and Daniel were left on their own.

Walking toward the starting line on Riverside by Auditorium Shores, Janet and Daniel were amazed at the carnival like atmosphere. Upbeat music was blasting from speakers in the starter's area; volunteers were handing out water, bananas, bandanas and paper fans. The Trojan Belle dance team from Anderson High School was performing for the crowd. Janet pinned Daniel's race number on his back, and he did the same for her. They slipped into the middle of the pack of runners just before the starter's gun went off.

Bang! The crowd surged forward, first at a jog, then breaking into a running pace. Janet felt a little awkward but was determined to run this race with Daniel. She glanced over at Daniel and he laughed. "Hey Mom, what's with the game face? It's called a fun run, smile!" Janet laughed, and relaxed a little, making her stride come more naturally. They ran side-by-side for the first two miles or so, and then Janet started to lag. She shouted to Daniel.

"Go on Daniel. Go ahead of me. Get your best time. Finish strong!"

"You sure Mom?"

"Yes, honey, I'll be right behind you."

Daniel sprinted ahead. Just before he was out of sight, he looked back and waved. Janet waved back and pushed forward. As Janet rounded the turn about a quarter of a mile before the finish line, she saw Daniel running back toward her.

"Daniel, what are you doing?"

"Mom, since I got you into this, I thought we should finish strong together. Come on, let's sprint to the finish line!"

Buoyed by his spirit, Janet sprinted with Daniel toward the finish line. Janet could tell that he was holding back a little to match her stride and she pushed herself harder to match his.

When they crossed the finish line, they cheered and hugged. Both got gold "winners" medals for finishing the race.

"You were right Daniel; that was fun. Thanks for coming back and spurring me along."

"No problem Mom, Reed men don't leave their women behind."

Daniel flashed a grin at Janet. This was a new side to Daniel, referring to himself as a man, being more protective of her. They were both slightly unsure of it. Middle school and adolescence were just around the corner. Little things had already started to change. He no longer held her hand in public. As her only child and constant companion, holding hands on outings had been second nature to them. At least they still had the tradition of reading together and tucking in at night.

Robert would grouse at Janet about it, when he was home at night. "The boy is ten years old. He doesn't need his mother to tuck him in at night!" Janet sometimes thought he was right but neither she nor Daniel was ready to give it up. The books and who did the reading had changed over the years, but it was still a special time of the day for both of them. Janet grabbed Daniel playfully and ruffled his hair.

"Okay, my little man, how about some ice cream?"

When they got home, Daniel hung his medal on the bulletin board in his room. Janet hung hers next to his.

"Mom, don't you want to hang that in your room? You earned it."

"Yes I did, but if I put it next to yours, it will always remind me of how we finished strong together."

Daniel slipped his arms around Janet and pressed his body against hers. Janet hugged him back.

"Best way to finish any race, right Mom?"

"Right Daniel."

Robert and Janet arrived back at the cottage just as Janet's memory was fading. Robert threw the car into park, opened his car door, and started to get out. Janet sat motionless in her seat; her eyes still closed. Robert sighed and turned back toward his wife.

"Janet, let's not fight. It's late. We're both tired. Maybe I overreacted. I suppose it wouldn't hurt for you to look into a dedication for Daniel. Find out about it, and then we'll talk. No promises though."

Janet opened her eyes and turned to face Robert. "Thank you." She turned back and reached for her door handle.

"By the way, did I mention that I will be gone overnight tomorrow night," Robert said, deftly changing the subject as they walked into the house.

"I don't think so."

"Well I've got to meet with Jack tomorrow in San Francisco and thought I'd just keep heading north to the retreat center in Napa Valley after the meeting. You know, get my thoughts together, practice my presentation, be fresh first thing in the morning. You're still welcome to come along if you want."

"We've already been over this, remember. We agreed that I would stay at the cottage when you went up to the directors' retreat in Napa. If you want to head out a night early that's okay. I'll be fine really. Besides, I told Melissa Allen that I would explore Half Moon Bay with her on Saturday."

"Okay then."

They went inside and crawled onto their respective sides of the king size bed, being careful not to disturb the blocks of evasion and illusion they had precariously stacked between them. Robert fell asleep trying to convince himself that the bench idea was a good thing. It was something concrete and constructive for Janet to focus on. Besides, it would keep her busy while he was away. And he needed some time alone.

CHAPTER 4

The church on the corner of Main and Poplar was an old, modest structure. It was made of wood, painted white, and had a traditional steeple with a copula and bell above the main entrance. Large, stained-glass windows depicting biblical scenes adorned the sides of the church. The historic plaque, situated next to the dark redwood doors, indicated that the church had been built in 1882 and was one of the few churches to survive the 1906 earthquake.

Another, clearly more modern structure, also painted white, adjoined the old church on the right side. The sign by the entrance of that building, said "Church Annex." Janet decided to start there.

Janet felt a little uneasy as she entered the church building. She had not been in a church since Daniel's funeral, which quite frankly, was still a bit of a blur to Janet. It's not like they had been big churchgoers anyway. They were more of the big event, holiday type churchgoers.

Robert and Janet were married at St. John's United Methodist Church and Daniel had his baptism and funeral there. Other than that, they attended church on Christmas, Palm Sunday, and Easter. In recent years, they didn't even go to their home church for the holidays. They would go to the church they thought had the best "holiday show"; ones with large choirs and talented guest musicians.

No one was in the entryway of the annex, so Janet wandered

down the hall toward the office doors. The first two doors that she came to were closed and the rooms were dark. The third door was ajar, and she heard activity inside. Janet knocked and pushed the door open slightly and peeked inside.

"Excuse me, I'm looking for a Pastor Paul Barnett."

A tall man, dressed in jeans and T-shirt, was bent over something in front of his desk, furiously tapping the side of it with a wrench. Janet stepped inside the office and spoke louder. "Excuse me, I'm looking for Paul Barnett."

The man looked up, put the wrench down and wiped his hands on the sides of his jeans. "Well you can stop looking, and I'll stop working. I could use a break anyway. I swear these instructions are written in Greek; and I only studied Latin in seminary." A large grin broke across his face as he extended his hand to Janet, "Hi, I'm Pastor Paul."

His eyes twinkled when he smiled. His features were classic Roman, with dark hair and eyes and a chiseled jaw line. Missy didn't tell me how handsome you are, Janet thought. Janet found herself smiling back at Pastor Paul as she leaned over to one side to see what he was building.

"That's my little project for Saturday's church bazaar," he explained. "I have to put together two massage chairs before tomorrow. You don't read Greek, do you?"

Janet laughed. "Massage chairs, now I see why this is a popular church!"

Pastor Paul chuckled, "The Lord works in mysterious ways. Actually, it's the fundraiser the youth group chose to do this year. I guess they were sick of car washes. One of the kids' mothers is a massage therapist and she's been giving the kids and me pointers on basic back massage techniques. What can I do for you today?"

"I'm Janet Reed. I'm visiting from Austin, Texas. Melissa Allen thought you might be able to help me with some information on a project I'm researching."

"Jack and Missy Allen are good friends of this church. Be happy to help if I can. Do you mind if I keep working while we talk?"

"No, not at all."

Paul picked up the wrench, knelt down behind the chair so that he was facing Janet and began fiddling with the nuts and bolts at the base of the chair. "So, are you a reporter or something?"

"Yes. No. Well, I mean not anymore. I used to be but that was years ago. I haven't worked as a reporter for a while." Janet felt uncharacteristically flustered around Pastor Paul. "This is a personal research project."

"Ok, so what is this project?"

"I hiked up to the cliff by the old lighthouse yesterday and saw the bench dedicated to Sarah Monroe. Missy Allen said that you were instrumental in getting that bench approved by the local government. I want to try and do something like that for my son who died recently."

Paul set the wrench down, wiped his hands on his jeans again, and strode over to Janet. He pulled the pair of office visitor chairs together and motioned for Janet to sit in one. He sat in the other and took Janet's hand in his.

"I am so sorry," he said, looking into Janet's eyes. "Please pardon my insensitivity. How long has it been since your son died?"

Janet met his eyes, and then looked down at the floor. She couldn't speak. It wasn't that he asked about Daniel's death, Janet was overwhelmed at the suddenness and intensity of his concern. Many people had expressed sorrow for Janet's loss; some heartfelt and some out of social correctness. It had been long enough now since Daniel's death that Janet thought she had become adept at dealing with both. But this man, this stranger, in one brief moment, touched her core with his caring act. Janet's eyes welled with tears. Pastor Paul reached over to his desk for some Kleenex with his free hand and gently laid them in Janet's lap.

"It's okay," Paul whispered. "We don't have to talk about it." He squeezed Janet's hand. She liked the strength and warmth she felt. Janet dabbed at her tears and looked up. Pastor Paul waited patiently for Janet to compose herself.

"I don't know what came over me," Janet began "I really don't cry in front of strangers like this…for no real reason. I mean Daniel has been dead for three months now. You'd think I would be …"

"Looping," Paul interrupted. "And it is perfectly natural. You can go along for months thinking you are handling the loss and then out of the blue, some little thing can set off your emotions, making it feel like you are going backward in your recovery. Looping is part of the grieving process and in the end, speeds your healing. Let's focus back on the bench, shall we?"

Janet smiled sheepishly at Paul. "Thank you, but I'm not sure I can remember my questions. Maybe I should come back another time. After all, you have those chairs to finish."

"Hey, I have an idea that will help us both. How about, you help me put the chairs together and if a question pops into your mind, you can ask it? That is if you have the time. Oh, and if you don't ask a question and help me anyway, I'll give you a free chair massage at the bazaar tomorrow."

"Sounds like an offer I can't refuse."

Janet spent the next hour and a half helping Pastor Paul assemble the massage chairs. He did most of the building. Her job was to navigate the instructions and hand him the requisite parts as he needed them. They worked in an awkward silence at first that quickly transformed into a comfortable quiet.

Everything he did seemed to put Janet at ease; the unhurried way he took the tools or chair parts from her; the thankful smile he flashed her every few minutes. Before long they were chatting about nothing in particular.

Janet found out that Paul grew up in Sacramento, California. He got a teaching degree from Berkeley and taught middle school for several years. He loved the outdoors; camping, hiking, bird watching;

anything to commune with nature. In fact, he was on a solo camping trip in Big Sur when he got "the call". Paul attended seminary near San Diego, and he has been the youth pastor at Trinity Church for almost four years. Although he didn't come out and say it directly, Janet gathered from his conversation and passion about the youth program that it had grown tremendously under his stewardship.

Janet told him about her past professional life as an investigative reporter and how she had given it up a few years after Daniel was born. Robert had started traveling more and it was getting harder to juggle her work schedule and take care of Daniel when she was alone. She told him a few of her favorite Daniel stories. Like the first time she took him trick-or-treating when he was two.

She had practiced with him for a whole week saying "Trick-or-Treat" when someone opened the door, and "Thank you" when they put candy in his bag. She told Paul how adorable he looked dressed up like one of the 101 Dalmatians, complete with droopy ears and droopy cheeks. The cheeks, she added, were Daniel's; the ears were shoulder pads from an old dress.

She was so proud that he shouted "Trick-or-Treat" when they arrived at the first house and watched him follow the lady's hand as she dropped two pieces of candy into his little pumpkin bucket. Janet waited patiently for him to say "Thank you" but he was still looking at the candy. "Daniel, what do you say?" she had prompted. A grin broke out across Daniel's face and he looked up at the lady and squealed excitedly "MORE!"

Paul got a good chuckle out of that one. Janet was glad. She treasured her memories of Daniel and didn't really have anyone to share them with, especially not Robert. Before long, the chairs were assembled. Paul and Janet stood back and admired their handy work.

"Not too shabby for a couple of novices. Janet, I can't thank you enough, you saved me hours of frustration. Hope I haven't kept you too long."

"It wasn't how I planned to spend my afternoon, but actually, I enjoyed it."

"Which reminds me," Paul said as he turned toward Janet, clasping her hands with his, "I guess I owe you a free massage tomorrow, since we never got to your questions about the bench."

"No, really, its okay, you don't have to."

"I insist, promise me you will stop by our massage booth tomorrow afternoon."

"Well, Missy and I are having lunch on Old Main Street tomorrow, which is just up the road, but I don't know if she'll want to come…"

"Of course she will, bring her along. You deserve some relaxation. Besides, I need to have someone to blame if the chairs break."

"Ah ha, the man has an ulterior motive." Janet said in mock surprise as she stepped back, releasing his hands. They both laughed.

"Seriously Janet, come on by, it's a fun event. I'll also try to pull together some information from my file on the bench approval process this evening that I can give you tomorrow."

"That would be nice," Janet said as she gathered her purse and headed toward the office door. She looked back over her shoulder at Paul as she was leaving and smiled. "I guess I'll see you tomorrow then."

CHAPTER 5

Robert arrived at the Seaside Inn just as the sun was setting. He had spent all day with Jack Allen, retooling the presentation for the board. It was ready. He was ready. It was time to relax.

Robert parked and went inside. A young couple sat drinking in the patio bar, watching each other more than the sunset. Robert felt a twinge of excitement as he always did on these overnight trips. He went into the bar before checking in, ordered a scotch on the rocks from the bartender and sat down at the table next to the couple.

Robert glanced at the couple next to him, as they ordered another round. He noticed that the young woman had slipped off her sandals and was running her toes under the edge of her companion's pant leg while he placed the order.

"Do you want to charge that to your room," the waiter asked the young man.

"Yes, room 208 please. And hey, can we see a menu?"

Robert sat back in his chair, sipped his scotch and watched the sunset. Yes, he thought, this will be a good night. When the waiter came back with the menus for his neighbors, Robert ordered another scotch and some fish tacos.

By the time Robert finished his third scotch, the two lovers had finished their food and were wrapped in each other's arms, whispering and laughing conspiratorially. Robert paid his tab and went to check in.

"Good evening sir, do you have a reservation?"

"No, I don't."

"That shouldn't be a problem; smoking or non-smoking?"

"Actually, it doesn't matter. Do you have a room available on the second-floor, say maybe 208 or 210?"

"Let's see. Room 208 is occupied, but 210 is available. It's a non-smoking room with a king size bed."

"Perfect, I'll take it."

Robert signed the registration form, picked up his key and went to his room to wait. After he entered the room, Robert immediately went to the window and gave it a tug. Yes, it opened. He had found over the years that the smaller inns usually had functioning windows. The sea breeze brushed past him, carrying with it the sounds of the night.

The anticipation was excruciating. It had been three months since he had allowed himself this guilty pleasure. He felt himself starting to get hard and tried not to think of what was about to happen. He thought about how it started, and he thought about Janet.

The passion had been gone from their marriage for years, more years than he cared to admit. After Daniel was born, and his job responsibilities increased, they just lost time and energy; and then over time, they lost interest. Truth was he liked to travel away from home overnight, especially after the first time it happened. If Janet knew how many times he'd volunteered for these trips, she would be angry, or worse, hurt.

In all the years of business travel he had never cheated on Janet, and Robert was proud of that fact. He knew many coworkers who bragged of their sexual conquests on business trips. In fact, some viewed Robert as a kill joy when he went to his room alone at the end of a night at the bars.

Then one night, while on a consulting trip in Myrtle Beach, it happened. He was staying at a small inn, a few blocks from the CEO's beach house. It had been a long, intense day. His presentation was not going well. He went to the bar, slammed down a few scotches and went to his room. All he wanted was a good night's sleep.

Robert had slipped into the bed at that inn, but his mind was still racing. He had opened the window, hoping that the sound of the Atlantic Ocean pounding the shoreline would lull him to sleep. He had just started to drift off to sleep when he heard a commotion in the room next door. The headboard of the bed in the next room was thumping against his wall.

What the hell, he thought, can't a guy get a decent night's sleep in this place! He banged on the wall and shouted for the couple to knock it off. They didn't follow his command. He listened as their love making became more intense.

The woman became very vocal, moaning and affirming his name. "Yes, yes Brad yes. Oh yes, Brad, Brad, yes!" Her voice was low and breathy.

Robert pounded on the wall again. "Hey, I'm trying to sleep over here!"

"Hey man, you might as well relax and enjoy it," Brad shouted back. "'Cuz we can't stop this rocket ship."

Robert heard the woman laugh briefly before the rhythmic thumping continued. Robert flopped back on his pillow, resigned to wait them out. When she started to moan, he figured that Brad had ratcheted it up a notch. He tried to image how they were doing it. That's when he figured out what Brad meant by "enjoy it." And he did, tremendously.

Every trip Robert went on over the next few months, he hoped to get a pair of boisterous lovers as neighbors. In fact, he craved it, but it didn't happen. Robert decided he couldn't wait for chance and devised a scheme to increase the probability. Hanging out in the bar before checking in had worked pretty well for him over the years. He had become more adept at picking the right couple over time as well.

Robert heard the young couple from the bar fumbling with the room key. He could sense their urgency, and his heart beat faster. The door closed. He heard snippets of giggling conversation, and then a window opening. Everyone loves a sea breeze. Robert swallowed hard; his palms were getting sweaty. It won't be long now. She was the right kind of woman. He knew it from the moment he spotted her at the bar.

The room next door became eerily quiet; the calm before the storm. Robert knew it well. Soon he could hear the rhythmic creaking of the bed. He felt himself rise under the sheets. He slid his hand down and slowly started to stroke himself. Pace yourself Buddy, Robert thought, you don't want to peak too soon.

Robert strained to hear the noises from the other room. He thought he could make out the rapid syncopated breath pattern that precedes the moaning. The breathing was getting louder and turning into full-fledged panting.

The young woman would soon be lost in the throes of animalistic pleasure, giving him the lubrication he needed to finish the job. Robert visualized her arching her back to receive maximum pleasure as the young man thrust himself deeper and deeper inside of her. She started to moan, first in a high pitch, then in guttural tones. Robert moaned with her as his stroke became faster and tighter.

They reached climax simultaneously. Both rooms fell silent, except for the faint sound of the pulsating waves. Robert sighed, rolled over on his side and drifted off to the best night's sleep he'd had since Daniel died.

CHAPTER 6

Janet watched the fog rolling in off the ocean as she sat on the deck sipping her coffee. She couldn't sleep and had risen early this morning. As it hit the desolate beach shoreline, the fog began to break up. By the time it reached the cottage deck, it was a translucent mist. It felt cool against her face. Still restless, Janet decided to hike back up to the lighthouse. She had hours before Missy was picking her up.

The view of the lighthouse in the fog from the beach was eerie. As it hit the cliffs, the fog ascended like whipped cream billowing from an aerosol can, silently pouring over the edge onto the land above; a clandestine invasion. Except for the rhythmic pulse of the beacon light, the lighthouse was virtually invisible.

Janet climbed the path up the cliff slowly. Visibility was decidedly worse here than at the cottage; maybe five to six feet at best. When she arrived at the top, Janet was startled to see the faint outline of a man sitting on the bench. She had not expected to see anyone up here this early. She considered turning around and heading back.

"Good Morning Ms. Reed. Are you also an admirer of mother nature's early morning ethereal display?"

"More of a fidgety insomniac," Janet replied recognizing Professor Briggs' voice, "but, I do agree, the fog up here is sublime, in a creepy sort of way." Janet sat down on the bench.

Professor Briggs chuckled. "The longer you live here the more you grow to love the fog. I find it more comforting than creepy."

Janet looked at the dedication inscription to Sarah on the bench again and remembered what Missy had told her the other night at dinner. "Do you mind if I ask you a question?" Janet began, looking up at Professor Briggs.

"Depends on the question."

"The other day when we met up here and you invited me to sit on the bench, did you think I was going to jump off the cliff?"

"That is an odd question, why do you ask?"

"A few nights ago I was having dinner in town with my husband's client's wife and I asked her about the history of this bench. She said you were originally against it because you didn't want to be on suicide watch, but that you were the one who came up with the poem for the inscription that seemed to end some controversy between the church and the county."

"I suppose that's true. What else did she say about me?"

"Only that you were a bit of a hermit and prefer to be addressed as Professor Briggs."

"I supposed that is also true, at least as far as the town's people are concerned. Tell me Ms. Reed, why are you so interested in this bench?"

"My son died three months ago, and I would like to do a similar tribute for him back in Austin."

"Ah, now I understand your original question, which I will still answer, if you answer this first - did you think you were going to jump off that cliff the other day?"

Janet paused for a moment and looked out at the fog drifting over the edge of the cliff. "Honestly, I don't know; I don't think I was thinking at all. I was just feeling the pull of the ocean. I'll be honest. I often wish I had died instead of Daniel. But then I think that if I die, he'll die a second death because there will be no one to keep his memory alive."

"Fair enough. I didn't think you were suicidal, just disturbed, and now I know why."

They sat in silence for a while, one observing and one absorbing the fog. Janet finally broke the silence. "Professor Briggs, I know we hardly know each other, but I do have another request, if it's not too much of an imposition."

"Well, if you're going to impose on me, I suppose you should call me Jonathon."

"Okay. And please call me Janet. I was wondering if you could help me select a poem for my son's bench. I'm not well versed in poetry. I mean, I know all of his favorite nursery rhymes, but he had just turned eleven when he died, and I think he would want something older and I want something more meaningful."

"I'm flattered but picking out a poem for someone is such a personal thing. I tell you what. Why don't you come up to my house and you can browse through my library. You can tell me about your son, and I might be able to suggest a few books you can borrow to look through at your leisure."

"That would be great. Thank you."

They walked up the hill to Jonathon's house. When they arrived, Jonathon held the door open for Janet and motioned for her to enter. The house was small but tidy. It was sparsely furnished except for the bookcase along the wall near the door, which was filled with books and nautical themed knick knacks. Jonathon offered to make some tea while Janet surveyed his poetry book collection.

"Impressive collection," Janet said when he returned with the tea.

"Yes, I do have a penchant for poetry."

Jonathon told Janet about the different styles and favorite themes of various poets. Janet spoke of Daniel's favorite activities, his rock collection and how he loved the outdoors. They decided Janet should take home an anthology of poems by Twentieth Century American Poets and a book of poems by Robert Frost to begin her search for a fitting poem for Daniel's memorial.

They sat down in two overstuffed leather easy chairs, which, together with an old oak coffee table, made up Jonathon's living room suite, and chatted as if they were old friends. Janet felt comfortable talking to Jonathon. He was a good listener and not judgmental.

Jonathon watched Janet as she talked about herself. He liked the way she could not keep her hands still when telling a funny story. He was glad that she smiled sometimes when she spoke of her son. He caught glimpses of a spark behind the veil of sadness. She was stronger than she knew, he thought, and prettier too. Jonathon now realized how much he missed a woman's companionship. Maybe it was time to open his heart again. It had been long enough.

Jonathon thought about Mai; her long silky black hair, her dark soulful eyes, her young supple body and her sunny smile. He still missed her. Over the years, Jonathon always gravitated to younger women. They made him feel vibrant and vital. But Mai was special. Despite their age and education differences, they had a real connection. He used to say that she had a poet's soul, to be so wise so young. She used to tease him that he had the heart of a lion, to be so strong so old.

Janet noticed the faraway look in Jonathon's eyes and figured she was talking too much about herself. She steered the conversation toward Jonathon and the local area. He told her that he graduated from Mississippi State and taught for a while at a several different colleges but spent most of his career teaching English at a private preparatory school for boys outside of Boston. Jonathon also recited the facts he knew about the history of the lighthouse.

At first, there was just a fog horn installed on the cliff in 1875, after several ships ran ashore near the point. It would blast over 1,000 hours per year to help ships get through the rain and dense fog. In the early 1900's a red glass oil lantern was added after there were several more wrecks. Then in 1927, the lighthouse was built, and a beacon installed.

The lighthouse was short by most standards, standing only around thirty feet tall, but that was good for keeping the light beam beneath the fog. A keeper manned the lighthouse until the early 1970's when an automated lighting system was installed. The keeper's house fell into disrepair and was eventually torn down.

According to Jonathon, this stretch of the San Mateo peninsula shoreline was used as a smuggling base during Prohibition for Portuguese and Italian fisherman who would take liquor up the coast to San Francisco's speakeasies. In fact, this particular lighthouse was important because it was the last lighthouse before Devil's Slide, eight miles up the coast. Devil's Slide is where bodies were routinely dumped during the rumrunners' wars of that time.

During World War II, military patrols based their operations from the lighthouse and kept a unit in the keeper's house. They patrolled the nearby beaches nightly, guarding against enemy invasions.

"You don't really get a sense of all that history, when you look inside the lighthouse. It really isn't much to look at." Jonathon concluded.

"You can get into the lighthouse?" Janet's eyes lit up. "I would love to see inside. I've been so curious." Janet looked at Jonathon with a hopeful smile.

"I must be a lonely old man," Jonathon mused, "to be so easily swayed by the smile of a pretty woman."

Janet blushed at his reference to her as a pretty woman. She looked down at the books in her lap momentarily and then back at Jonathon. What was going on with her lately?

"Don't tell me you're not used to hearing that?" Jonathon teased. "Why your husband should be horsewhipped, if he doesn't tell you daily how pretty you are. Of course, I'm not one who should be dispensing marital advice. At least he snagged you; I think I'm destined to be a bachelor forever."

"Oh, I don't know about that, Professor. You're a distinguished scholar, a good conversationalist, a gentleman, and believe me, there are far too few of those around today, and on top of all that, you make a mean cup of tea!"

"You left out handsome," Jonathan joked as he stood up and offered his arm to Janet. "Shall we proceed to the lighthouse my dear?"

"I would be delighted." Janet said, making a mock curtsey before taking his extended arm.

On the way out of the house, they stopped at the bookcase where Jonathon opened a decorative wooden box and took out a small cylindrical tool.

"What's that?" Janet asked.

"The key"

"Odd looking key."

"True, but very functional in the right hands."

When they reached the lighthouse, Jonathon pulled the tool from his pocket and started fiddling with the slender levers on the end. He inserted the levered end into the lock and after a few twists back and forth, the lock clicked, and Jonathon pushed the door open.

"Where did you learn that trick?" Janet asked.

"Let's just say I wasn't always a distinguished scholar."

Janet laughed. "So, who has the real key to this place?"

"A few people on the county maintenance crew," Jonathon answered. "Believe it or not, they used to keep a key hidden in a fake rock over in that pile of rocks about ten feet from the entrance."

"That doesn't sound very secure."

"Well, probably not, but they didn't know I knew about it and it made it easier for the maintenance crew to come check on things and not worry about who had the key. Besides, not many people come up here. There are other lighthouses in the area that have been maintained better and are open to the public for tours. Most people visit those."

"So, what happened to that key?"

"I haven't been able to find it since Sarah's death. I figured the county crew took it back because there were a lot of curiosity seekers that came up here for awhile after her death and they didn't want anyone to stumble across it." Jonathon motioned toward the open door, "Shall we go in?"

The inside of the lighthouse was dark and dingy. The fog had lifted so the mid-morning sunlight streamed down from the windows above, making it look like a dungeon. The base of the lighthouse was empty except for an old wooden crate in the back and a circular metal staircase in the center which led to the beacon's watch room.

Several stairs at the top of the staircase were missing, making it difficult, if not impossible to reach the watch room. Janet walked up as far as she could and contemplated how to access the top.

"Do you think the railing is sturdy? Maybe I can skinny up it to reach the top," Janet asked Jonathon. "Or, maybe you could give me boost?" Janet looked over her shoulder at Jonathon and smiled coyly.

Jonathon shook his head. "Don't think that's a good idea. The trouble is not getting up there, it's getting back down. Last time I helped a young lady up there, she nearly broke her neck and mine getting back down and she was a lot younger than either of us."

Janet turned around and looked at Jonathon. "What young lady? Sarah? I thought you said you didn't know her?"

"I said I didn't know her well." Jonathon answered. Jonathon sat on the bottom step and looked over at the crate in the corner. "In fact, I think the longest conversation we ever had took place inside this lighthouse. A sudden rain storm had come up and caught us both in it. I was on my way back from a walk when I saw her huddled against the lighthouse, trying to stay dry. I offered to let her come up to my house until the storm passed but she declined.

I remembered about the hide-a-key and asked her if she wanted to wait out the storm inside the lighthouse. She cautiously agreed. I let her in, and she sat over there on the crate, soaking wet. She looked a little nervous, so I sat here on this step and we started talking about poetry and writing.

Eventually she warmed up and showed me some of hers. Most of it was pretty dark stuff for a young girl, but powerful. She really had some potential. Soon, she opened up a little more and started talking about how hard it was to feel at home in a new place. I sympathized with her. I hadn't been here much longer than she had.

Then she became curious about the watch room and the lantern room. She asked me for a boost. I obliged. She loved the view from up there, but, like I said, nearly killed us both getting down.

She stopped by my cottage one afternoon not long after that rainy day to look at some of my books. That was just about a month before she died. Only saw her in passing on the lighthouse cliff a few times after that."

Janet watched Jonathon as he looked at the empty space above the crate and sensed that he missed the girl. Maybe he wanted a protégé or really was just an old softie. "Okay, I can take a hint. I won't climb all the way up there. How about I just stand on the rail and look over the top for a minute? You can hold my legs steady."

"Did you ever hear the expression, 'curiosity killed the cat'?" Jonathon answered.

"Luckily, I'm not a cat and I have pretty good balance." Janet stood on the top step and did one of her yoga balancing poses. "Tada."

"Where did you learn that trick?" Jonathon asked.

"Let's just say I wasn't always a stay-at-home Mom."

Jonathon laughed and walked up the steps to hold her legs. Janet climbed up on the rail and peered over the edge into the watch room. Jonathon had been right, Janet thought, this room is really not much to look it.

It was quite barren with just a small wooden table pushed up against the wall with a solitary chair. There was a shelf on the other side which housed an old lantern, some light bulb containers, a few tools and plenty of cobwebs. A small staircase led to the lantern room.

"I sure wish I could see the view from the lantern room." Janet said.

"Peeking over the edge only, that was our deal."

"You're right, safety first." Janet stretched up on her tiptoes to do one last scan before climbing off the railing. Just as she was about to turn around and climb down, she saw something wedged behind one of the table legs, against the wall. It looked like some sort of ledger or notebook. Janet tried to stretch further to get a better look.

"Ok now, Janet, unless you know a levitation trick, that's far enough." Jonathon cautioned.

The notebook was dusty, but Janet was pretty sure it was blue. Janet decided not to mention what she had seen to Jonathon. She had been trained not to reveal a hunch until it had been confirmed. She would have to find a way to get back in here later, alone. Jonathon held Janet's hand as she climbed down.

"You were right," Janet said, "There really wasn't much to see. Thanks for indulging me though."

"My pleasure."

Janet looked at her watch. "Yikes look at the time. Someone is supposed to pick me up at the cottage in ten minutes!" Janet thanked Jonathon for the tour and the books and headed down the cliff to the beach.

CHAPTER 7

Janet arrived at the cottage just as Missy was pulling up.

"Sorry," Janet explained as she let herself and Missy into the cottage, "I lost track of the time. I was visiting with Professor Briggs about poetry for Daniel's bench. He gave me a few books to look through." Janet tossed the books on the table and headed toward the bedroom. "I'll just be a few minutes. A speedy shower and a quick change and I'll be right out."

"Take your time." Missy looked at the books on the table and shook her head. "Boy, when you get an idea in your head, you really go after it."

Janet stuck her head out the bedroom door and said apologetically, "Yeah, I guess I can be a little Type A sometimes."

Missy laughed. "Honey, with husbands like ours, being a little Type A is a walk in the park."

The ten-minute drive from the cottage to Half Moon Bay was spectacular. Missy drove her BMW M3 convertible along Cabrillo Highway with the top down. The sky was blue, the air was crisp, and Janet had a clear view of the Pacific Ocean and its rugged shoreline the whole way. Missy parked by City Hall on Main Street.

Janet could see why Missy liked to hang out here. Main Street in Half Moon Bay is full of historic structures, ranging from a one hundred and fifty-year-old redwood house built by the son of a Mexican ranchero, to the City Hall housed in an old bank building built in 1922. There is even an old school bell on one corner. Like most historic districts in resort towns, the street was lined with unique, high-end boutiques, cafes, craft stores and galleries.

Janet and Missy spent the first hour popping in and out of the plethora of shops. When Janet mentioned she was hungry, Missy said they had to stop at the Moonside Bakery and Café for lunch. "They have the best curry chicken and apple sandwiches and a tiramisu to die for."

After lunch, they wandered through some galleries. Missy knew which ones served wine to their customers. Janet suspected that not all customers were served wine when they visited the galleries; just ones that the gallery owners knew were big spenders. Missy told Janet that she had bought all the artwork for the cottage and most of the pieces for her home in Half Moon Bay. "The northern half of the San Mateo coastline is populated by brilliant artisans," Missy had said. "I love supporting the local artists when I can."

Missy took Janet on a short detour off Main Street to show her the old town jail built in 1911. It was a small, square, white stucco building with two large wooden green doors and two tall windows at the front. Inside there were two tiny cells and a tiny office. Janet and Missy had a snapshot taken of themselves in one of the cells. "We're out together one day and we end up in the slammer," Missy joked.

"Robert will be so proud," Janet chuckled. She felt light-hearted today. It was good to be out and doing things again. She was also looking forward to seeing Pastor Paul.

"Oh, Missy, I promised Pastor Paul that we would drop by the Church bazaar this afternoon. Do you mind?"

"Oh no, of course not, it'll be fun. I forgot they were having it today. So, I guess that means you met with him this week."

"Yes, yesterday. I ended up helping him put together some massage chairs for the bazaar."

"That figures, he always finds a way to get everyone involved. Okay let's head over there. It's just a few blocks from here."

Janet and Missy meandered through the bazaar to the chair massage station.

"Welcome ladies," Pastor Paul said, as he came out from behind one of the chairs. He smiled broadly as they approached.

"He's such a charmer." Missy whispered, "All the girls in the youth group have a crush on him. And, if truth be told, so do their mothers."

"Well, Mrs. Reed, I see you couldn't resist my offer."

"Call me Janet, please."

"Ok Janet, step right up and we'll test this chair you helped me build." He made a sweeping gesture with his hand and ushered Janet into the chair. "You too, Missy. Tim here has been waiting to work on his next victim… I mean customer… and all for a good cause too."

They all laughed, and the two women settled into the twin massage chairs. At the first touch of Pastor Paul's hands on her shoulders, Janet tensed up more. Paul gently leaned over and whispered in her ear, "Janet, I want you to take a deep breath and let it go, then close your eyes and imagine the sound of the surf. I will do the rest."

Janet followed his instructions and felt herself soften and sink into the chair. "That a girl," Pastor Paul said as he began kneading the muscles around her neck. He worked his way slowly down her back and then up again to her shoulders. His touch was firm yet gentle. Every now and then his body would brush up against her back or her thigh as he worked. Janet felt a tingle pulse through her body each time it happened. How long has it been, she wondered, since a man's touch made her feel that way? She couldn't remember.

Certainly Robert hadn't made her feel that way in many years. They still made love occasionally, but it was more out of habit, than passion. One of them would realize that it had been many months since they had had sex and make some fumbling move after they got into bed, usually after they had both been drinking. It was always the same, very perfunctory. Foreplay was dispatched with quickly. Janet used to joke that Robert spelled it "fourplay", since it seemed to last only about four minutes before Robert was ready for the main event.

Janet was engaged enough to meet his physical needs. There had been little or no emotion involved in their lovemaking for years. She had sex with him more out of a sense of duty than love. She hoped it would be over quickly. It always was. They would drift off to sleep, Robert relieved physically, Janet relieved mentally.

They had made love once since Daniel died, early on when the grief was raw. Ironically, it was the most passionate either one of them had been in years. The next morning they both felt awkward about it and slipped back into their separate grief hollows. Neither had let the other in again.

Janet felt Pastor Paul's hands caressing the nape of her neck. Periodically, he would run his fingers tenderly through her hair. Janet was at once glad and sorry that this massage was taking place at such a public place. Pastor Paul removed his hands from her neck and gently patted her back. "Okay Janet, times up. That's your reward for all your hard work yesterday." Pastor Paul helped Janet climb out of the massage chair.

"Wow, that was great," Janet gushed, a little too enthusiastically, she reprimanded herself silently.

"Don't mention it."

Missy joined them. "I think I ended up taking a little nap during my massage. I don't know if it was Tim's technique or the wine at the galleries." Everyone laughed.

"So what major conglomerate is Jack trying to conquer this week?" Pastor Paul teased Missy.

"Oh who knows," Missy replied, "I can't keep up with them all. In fact, he's at a board retreat this weekend where Janet's husband is proposing some merger or acquisition deal."

"Does that mean you two lovely ladies are on your own tonight? Why don't you have dinner with me? I'm certainly not going to feel like cooking after working this booth all afternoon."

"Sorry, I'm going to have to take a rain check. I promised Mother I would pick up the kids by 6:00," Missy replied. Missy wished she could take back that last sentence as soon as she said it. She looked over at Janet and then at Pastor Paul. He was already looking at Janet and smiling like everything was fine. He's good, Missy thought.

"Well Janet, that just leaves the two of us. What do you say? I hate eating alone."

"I don't know," Janet started.

"Say, I have a great idea," Pastor Paul cut in, "I can bring the file on the memorial bench and we can discuss any questions you have over dinner. Kill two birds with one stone, so to speak." He gave Janet a posed pleading look.

Janet grinned. "Ok, ok, I'll go. It doesn't look like you are going to take no for an answer, anyway."

"He never does," Missy said.

"Great. I'll pick you up around 7:00. Where are you staying?"

"At the Allen's cottage, off of Reef Point Road."

"Ok, I'll pick you up there. Missy, have a safe ride home and tell Jack 'hello' for me."

CHAPTER 8

Pastor Paul and Tim finished loading the last massage chair into his office. "Thanks Tim, I'll see you tomorrow," Paul said as he sat down at his desk. He leaned back in his chair and put his feet up on his desk, interlacing his hands behind his head. He was tired. He was accustomed to putting in long hours at the church; comes with the job, he knew that. It's just that lately, the work hours had become more of a strain, and the work more of a chore. He needed a break. He should put in for vacation before the holiday season arrives. This is a great time of year to go camping along the coast.

Paul looked up at the clock and noticed that he only had one hour until he was supposed to pick up Janet. No rest for the weary. But dinner tonight would not be a chore. He was attracted to Janet; he couldn't deny that. He sensed that she was attracted to him as well; and he had good instincts when it came to women.

Early on in his career, Paul realized that his pastoral position made him more attractive, and available, to many women. Some just liked to flirt. Some were so enamored with him that they could barely speak in his presence. And others were down right aggressive, especially the divorced moms. All of them would do whatever he asked them to do. He never lacked for volunteers.

When he first arrived at Trinity, Paul wrestled with the ethics of dating women from the church. Then, he decided to date one of the divorced moms. After all, he had rationalized; she was single, attractive and actively pursuing him. Besides, he spent so much time at the church, where else was he going to meet women? It ended badly. She wanted a father for her son. He wanted a more casual relationship. She complained to Pastor Harrington and left the congregation. He was more careful after that, choosing women who needed to be discreet, for one reason or another.

Paul remembered that he promised to bring the memorial bench file to share with Janet. He reached over and unlocked the bottom desk drawer, where he kept his private files. He grabbed a large file from the back of the drawer and tossed it on his desk. Paul opened it and began flipping through it, book marking selected items to share with Janet.

When he reached the back of the file, he grinned. "The bible may say 'love your enemies'", Paul said out loud, "but Sun Tzu said, 'If you know the enemy and know yourself, you need not fear the results of a hundred battles.'" I don't know you, Paul thought, but I know your type and I know your Achilles heel. Don't cross me again, Professor. Paul pulled out the sub file entitled "Jonathon Briggs" and put it back in the drawer.

Paul smugly thought back about his last encounter with Professor Briggs. Following a San Mateo County Board of Supervisor's Planning Committee meeting, where Professor Briggs had testified against the bench, Paul approached him outside in the parking lot.

"Excuse me Professor Briggs," Paul began. "May I have a word with you? I'm Pastor Paul from Trinity Church."

"Yes, I know who you are."

"This bench is important to the church's youth group. They want to honor Sarah's memory."

"Why can't they do that at the church?"

"The cliff was special to Sarah. It was her favorite place. They want to make this about her, not the church. I heard your testimony in there and, quite frankly, I don't understand why you should care."

"At least I am not acting out of guilt."

"What are you implying?"

"Interpret it however you want."

"What I want is for you to stop opposing the bench, Professor."

"I don't like being told what to do."

"Neither do dead men."

"What do you mean by that?"

"Interpret it however you want, but just know that I know, and I will be watching your every move."

CHAPTER 9

The telephone rang just as Janet was getting out of the shower. It was 6:30. Janet knew it would be Robert. When he was away on business trips, his pattern was to call every other day, right before dinnertime; whether he needed to or not, Janet often joked to herself. Janet picked up the phone.

"Hi Honey. How's the big meeting going?" Janet used to wonder why she still called Robert "honey". She decided it was just part of the game they played; the "we are happily married" game. And, after all, even though they weren't really in love anymore, she did care for him.

Besides, it is not like "honey" was a special nickname she used only for Robert. She called lots of people "honey", her sisters, nieces and nephews, Daniel's friends, and any little kids she wanted to address but didn't know their name. It was just a habit; a good ole Texas habit. She didn't call Daniel "honey" though. He was her "Sweet Boy". That was the first thing she called him when he was placed into her arms after delivery and the nickname just stuck.

"Great, the meeting is going great. My presentation was well-received. We're heading out for cocktails and dinner soon to socialize and give the board members a chance to ask questions in a less structured setting. The formal vote on the merger is tomorrow. Jack and I both feel they will go for it. So, did you and Missy have a fun day?"

"Yes, we had a good time. She really is a hoot, especially after a few glasses of wine. She just left to go back to San Francisco an hour ago."

"That's great Janet. Glad to hear that. What are you going to do tonight?" Robert never called Janet by any nickname. She didn't notice that until after they had been married a few years.

"Oh, just a little research on the memorial bench." Which was the truth, Janet rationalized later, just not the whole truth.

"Ok, well don't work too hard. Hey, Jack's here, I've got to go. I'll see you tomorrow night."

"Alright, good luck with the vote."

"Thanks."

Janet hung up the phone knowing that Robert was in his element. He lived for nights like this. He was on the verge of sealing a deal, sharing good food, fine scotch, and his expert opinion with corporate big shots. He would be high on life and high on himself by the end of the night. Janet wondered what type of nights she lived for anymore. She thought about the possibilities tonight might bring, then, quickly put the thought out of her mind. It is just a friendly business dinner.

When Pastor Paul arrived, Janet was just putting the finishing touches on her make-up. She had changed her clothes three times before settling on the white capri pants and turquoise, sleeveless, v-necked, knit top that she now wore. Janet stopped and looked at herself in the mirror one more time. She still had a good figure. The yoga helped, but really, she was just blessed with a good metabolism and didn't have to work too hard to keep the weight off. She practiced a smile in the mirror, grabbed the sweater that matched her top and went to answer the door.

Pastor Paul drove them to the Half Moon Bay Brewing Company, which, as Paul pointed out to Janet, is not actually in Half Moon Bay, but in Princeton-by-the-Sea. It is the only brew pub on the San Mateo coast and overlooks the Pillar Point Harbor.

Paul thought it would be a fun and relaxing spot for dinner. A great view of the ocean and some live music might also help put Janet in the right mood, if she was at all receptive to his charms this evening. Paul knew he had to be careful. It's not so much that Janet was married, but that she was married to a business associate of Jack Allen's. Paul did not want to get on Jack Allen's bad side, or Missy's either for that matter. They had too much money and influence in the church. No, if they did anything, he would have to make sure they did not get caught.

There was a band playing on the outdoor patio, so they decided to sit outside. Paul chose a table at the edge of the patio, with a view of the ocean. They ordered a couple of beers.

Janet looked around. "This is really a great place," she said, "Good choice."

"Thanks, I like to come here to unwind, when I get the chance, which is not very often."

"Sounds like the youth program keeps you very busy."

"That's an understatement! But, and I know this may sound cliché, it really is rewarding to work with teenagers; young minds and bodies on the brink of coming into their own; forming their own identities, their future. I really love being a part of that process.

They have so much energy and fresh perspectives. And when you find one who is troubled or has lost her way, it's even more fulfilling when you can reach out to her and give her hope and direction again."

Janet watched Pastor Paul as he spoke. He is so passionate, so committed. She longed for someone to feel that way about her. She wondered why he had never married and had kids of his own. In a way, she guessed he was married to his job, just like Robert. Somehow, it seemed different with Pastor Paul. Janet glanced at the folder on the table and wondered if Pastor Paul was referring to Sarah with his last comment.

"Did Sarah lose her way?"

Pastor Paul hesitated for a moment. He saw Janet glance at the file. "That's the sad thing about Sarah. She was a lost soul when she moved here, but she was finding her way when the accident happened." This was not how Paul wanted to spend the evening. He had to get business over with and get Janet to relax, to open up. "Hey, this is a business dinner, right?"

"Right."

"Then, I say, let's take care of business and then have dinner. It will do us both some good to have some time to just kick back." He slid his chair over next to Janet's and opened the file. "I have bookmarked some pages that I thought might contain the type of information you are looking for."

Pastor Paul took Janet through the steps he took to get the bench installed; from design to manufacturers to county permits and lobbying the commissioners for approval. "As it turns out, something I thought would be a simple memorial turned into a division of church and state issue. Initially, I didn't think it would be a problem, until someone from the public opposed the bench."

"You mean Professor Briggs?"

"Yes, how did you know?"

"Missy told me."

"Well, anyway, he opposed the bench in general and also raised the issue of the use of our planned biblical quote on a bench on public property. I eventually convinced him to drop his opposition to the bench. I think he would have consented to the use of a biblical passage too, but, by then, the issue had already been pointed out to the county commissioners and they didn't want to raise the ire of any other citizens. However, I don't foresee that being a problem for you, unless you want to use a biblical passage on the bench in the city park you spoke of."

Janet shook her head in agreement. "No, I don't think that will be a problem for me. But I do want to say that I think the poetry quote on Sarah's bench is very moving and profound for the location."

"Yes, I would have to agree, if we couldn't have scripture, it was a good verse. Obviously, the county commissioners thought so too. And, as Missy probably told you, credit goes to Professor Briggs for that quote." Paul knew that Missy was a gossip. It was one of the reasons he continued to delicately fend off Missy's flirtatious advances.

Janet gazed at Pastor Paul and smiled. She was on her second beer and feeling more than a little appreciative. "Thank you so much Pastor Paul, for taking the time to help me wade through all of this information. I know it will make the process so much easier for me in Austin."

Paul reached over and squeezed Janet's hand. "Don't mention it. I am happy to assist you any way I can. By the way, for the rest of the evening, I am just 'Paul'. I think I am officially off duty." Paul leaned back in his chair, stretched out his legs, and sighed.

Janet smiled and squeezed his hand back. "Okay Paul." Just then their dinners arrived, and Paul put the file away under his chair. He did not move his chair back to the other side of the table. They ate their dinners and made small talk. Paul ordered another round of beers.

After dinner, Paul coaxed Janet out onto the dance floor. The band was playing oldies from the 80's. The music took Janet back to her college years. She felt carefree. Janet and Paul danced until the band took a break. They slumped into their chairs, exhausted but laughing.

"Oh my God," Janet said, "That was so much fun. You, Paul, are a very good dancer." Janet, even in her tipsy state, realized what she had just said in front of a pastor. "Oh, sorry," she continued, "about the 'oh my God' thing, bad habit."

Paul laughed. "Don't worry about it. I'm off duty, remember."

Now that they were off the dance floor, Janet felt the full force of the cool ocean breeze. She pulled her sweater tighter around her. Paul put his arm around her and pulled her closer to him to help keep her warm. Janet put her head on his shoulder. She knew she shouldn't, but it just felt like the natural thing to do. They sat there for a moment, watching the waves, letting the ocean breeze refresh them. Paul finally spoke. "It's getting late. I think it's time to get you home."

Paul walked Janet to the front door of the cottage. There was an awkward silence. Janet purposefully fumbled with the key to buy some time. She wanted to ask him in but wasn't sure if she would regret it if she did.

"Thank you for a wonderful evening," she finally said.

"Will I see you at church tomorrow?" Paul asked.

"To be perfectly honest, I am not much of a church goer."

"Trinity is different from most churches. Come to the 9:30 service. It's our folk service. There's guitar music, no formal liturgy and a lot of lay participation. It's very casual. You don't even have to dress up. Most of our congregation under 40 prefers this service. Besides, I'm giving the sermon tomorrow and it will be more inspired if I look out from the pulpit and see you."

Janet blushed. Paul pulled her closer to him. As he hugged her, he nuzzled his nose into her neck, inhaling the scent of her perfume. His right hand drifted from her shoulder to her head. Janet felt her resolve weaken. He gently tugged at her hair and she let her head fall back into his hand. She looked up at him as he bent down to kiss her.

They kissed for several minutes; moist, jalapeno jelly kisses, sizzling, sweet and soft. Paul's grip around Janet's waist became tighter. Janet began to feel that she couldn't breathe. She pulled back a little to catch her breath and figure out what she should do next.

"Boy, what you won't do to get a person to come to church on Sunday," Janet said with a nervous laugh.

Paul sensed her uncertainty. "Janet, I'm sorry, I shouldn't have. I don't know what came over me. I…"

Janet placed her index finger over his lips. "No, it's a.., it's okay, really. See you at church tomorrow."

Janet smiled at Paul and went inside. She leaned against the inside of the door, closed her eyes, and listened to his car pull out of the driveway. She had done the right thing, but she already regretted it.

CHAPTER 10

Pastor Paul's kisses still lingered on Janet's lips when she awoke on Sunday. She had tossed and turned half the night, alternately thinking of what could have been with Paul and how she was going to get back into the lighthouse and get that notebook. By the time she finally drifted off to sleep, Janet had decided on two things. First, she would attempt to get the notebook first thing in the morning. Second, if she ever got another chance to make love with Paul, she was going to jump at it.

The sky was already starting to get light as Janet pulled on her jeans and jacket. She knew Professor Briggs got up early for his morning walk. If she timed it right, she could get into the lighthouse while he was on his walk. If she missed her opportunity this morning, she would have to wait until the late afternoon, around the time she first met him. That would be riskier. There could be other people around and more visibility.

It was not as foggy this morning as yesterday, but there was still enough to make it easy to sneak around and not be seen. She hurried along the beach and climbed halfway up the cliff to the lighthouse. She spotted a grove of trees and slipped behind them and waited. She hoped he would be on schedule. She didn't have a lot of time. She had promised Paul she would be at the 9:30 service this morning.

Janet heard someone coming down the cliff. It had to be Professor Briggs. She didn't know of anyone else who lived up at the top. Most of the houses were down along the beach where Missy and Jack's cottage was. She pressed herself against the far side of the largest tree, craning her head around slightly to watch him pass. Yes, it was Professor Briggs and he had not seen her.

As soon as he was out of sight, she scurried up the cliff and raced up the path to his house. Her plan was to sneak into his house, get the key tool, run to the lighthouse, open the door, climb up into the watch room, snatch the notebook, climb down and return the tool before he returned from his morning walk. Yesterday he said he walked for an hour each morning, so there should be plenty of time if she moved quickly.

She reached the front door and turned the knob. It was locked. Rats, she hadn't figured him the type to lock the front door. She would have to break in. She went around to the side of the house and tugged at a few windows. They didn't budge. She went to the back. The back door was also locked, but the kitchen window was open slightly. That would have to do.

She pulled off the screen and pushed the window open. As she climbed in she hoped he did not have dishes in the sink. Breaking a dish was not part of the plan. Her heart was racing now. She would have liked to say that she had never broken into a house before. But that wouldn't be true. Although, technically, it was an office she broke into when working on the Unexco nursing home scandal story.

She was a young reporter then, a little too eager. After letting herself into the office, she found the information she needed for the story, but when the editor found out how she got it, he wouldn't print it; unless she could find other sources to cite for the information she "discovered".

She had been crestfallen, but only temporarily. She quickly learned another lesson. It is a lot easier to get people to give you information if you already know what you want them to say. So, in the end, she got her sources and her story was published.

That story helped to propel her career. She had been a good reporter. Her editor was sad to see her go when she left to be a full-time mom to Daniel. She used to wonder if she had made the right decision. After last spring, she knew she had. Maybe she would go back to it again, when she was ready.

Janet climbed in. Luckily, the sink was empty; good old tidy Jonathan. Janet made her way to the bookcase and opened the box on the shelf and took out the "key". She had watched him closely yesterday and was pretty sure she could replicate the pattern of the levers.

She unlocked his front door and slipped out. She made a mental note to relock the door after she returned his tool. At the lighthouse, she quickly arranged the levers and tried to open the lock. It didn't turn at all. She closed her eyes and tried to envision the lever arrangement. She rearranged the levers and tried again. Nothing. Be patient, she told herself. You can do this. After a few more false starts, the lock finally tumbled. She was inside.

She placed Jonathan's tool in her pocket and climbed up the circular metal staircase as far as she could. She hopped up on the rail and reached overhead, grabbing the edge of the watch room floor. She inched upwards along the rail as far as she could go. Her shoulders were now level with the floor. Okay, this is it, Janet thought. Let's see if doing all those chaturangas in yoga is going to pay off.

Janet took a deep breath and jumped. As she did so, she used her arms to push her torso up onto the floor above. Once her body was firmly on the floor, she swung her legs up. Janet stood up and caught her breath. Not too shabby for someone who is almost forty, she thought.

She walked over to the table and cautiously reached for the notebook. She did not want to disturb a nest of spiders or worse. She wondered if they had scorpions in California. You do not reach blindly into a dark, dusty space in Texas.

Janet pulled at the top corner of the notebook, until it fell out from behind the table leg. Good, nothing else moved. She picked up the notebook and dusted it off on her pants. Without hesitating, she opened the cover. On the first page there were several intricate doodles and what looked like someone practicing a signature. She moved closer to the watch room windows to get a better look. Janet stared incredulously at the page. There, in cursive, written over and over again was "Sarah Monroe".

She snapped the book shut and clutched it to her chest. "Holy shit, this is the missing notebook," she muttered to herself. She stared out the window, as her mind churned over what she should do with the book. Should she give it to the authorities? Should she give it to Sarah's mom? Should she tell Jonathon? Should she tell Paul? There was no question in her mind, however, that no matter which actions she chose, she was going to read it first.

Out of the corner of her eye, Janet saw someone start to climb up the cliff path to the lighthouse. Her heart stopped. Damn. He took a shorter walk today. Janet tucked the notebook in the back waistband of her jeans, under her coat, and hurried to the edge of the broken staircase.

She looked down. It would be very bad if she missed the staircase, possibly fatal. There wasn't a yoga move that could help her with this. She could try a straight jump onto the top step but that might be dicey, especially since the stairs were narrow and circular. Glancing over her shoulder out the window, Janet realized that she didn't have time to consider any more; Professor Briggs was halfway up the cliff.

Janet acted on instinct, letting her inner tomboy take over. She leaped toward the rail with her hands outstretched; catching the rail like it was a rung on the monkey bars. The momentum of the jump swung her around over the top. She held on tight and hooked her legs around the rail as she came back down. Janet hung there for a second but didn't allow herself the luxury of more time.

She slid down the rail hand over hand until she felt safe to unhook her legs and step onto the staircase. She ran down the stairs and peeked outside. No sign of Professor Briggs. Janet took the tool out of her pocket and relocked the door.

Professor Briggs crested the top of the cliff just as she slipped behind the lighthouse. He headed for the bench. Janet thought about her next move. She had to get back to his house before he did. She had to return the key tool to his box and relock his front door. Could she sneak up the path to his house while he sat on the bench? He seemed so aware of everything around him. She had to try.

Janet skirted along the far side of the cliff, trying to stay out of the line of sight of the bench and Professor Briggs for as long as possible. If she could just make it to the woods at the edge of the path to his house, she would be safe. She could slip up through the woods on the side of the path and put everything back the way it was. She had about ten more yards to go before she reached the woods. All of it was in plain sight of the bench. If he turned around, he would see her. She hoped he was being hypnotized by the waves.

Janet desperately wanted to make a dash for the woods, but she knew she would make too much noise and be discovered if she did. So, she took a deep breath and walked as quickly as she could while still being quiet. When she reached the woods, she looked back over her shoulder. Professor Briggs was still looking at the ocean, but he was now standing. Shit, Janet thought. He's going to head home. She hurried through the woods toward his house. At least he had not seen her yet.

Janet slipped in through his front door and quickly turned the lock. She peeked through the window and saw Professor Briggs walking briskly up the path. She figured she had about two minutes lead time. That should be enough. She hustled over to the bookcase and placed the tool in its box. She quickly scanned the bookcase. Nothing looked out of place. She headed to the kitchen and climbed out the window. She lowered the window just as he arrived at the front door.

Jonathon put the key in the lock and turned it until it clicked. He hesitated a moment, as he always did, before opening the door. As he started to enter, he heard a noise from the back of the house. He froze, listening for another sound.

Jonathon Briggs had dreaded this day. The day they came to capture him. He wasn't sure who would find him first, the F.B.I. or the Pham organization. The former would put him in jail, but the latter, he shuddered to think about it. They wouldn't kill him right away. He knew that. He still had information they wanted.

Twice a day he patrolled, looking for signs of their presence. He had never seen any. He had started to think they had given up; that he was safe at last; that the plan handed to him by fate had worked. Nothing seemed out of place this morning on his walk. But then again, he had let his guard down lately.

He had been preoccupied with thoughts of a full life again; a life that included a lady; a life where he could move freely about the community. He had carefully laid the foundations here. He was reclusive, but not eccentrically so. He was polite and proper in town when he shopped but didn't really socialize with any of the locals.

His main conversations in the past year had been with the occasional tourist and Sarah. Sarah's death complicated his plan. Ironically, it was his academic reputation in the community and his perceived candor about Sarah's visits to the cliff that got him off the hook with the police, at least for awhile.

Pastor Paul had made some unpleasant insinuations when he opposed the bench. But then, Paul Barnett does not know what he thinks he knows, and he certainly does not know Jonathon Briggs.

He shouldn't have opposed the bench in the first place; it brought too much attention to him. It was a momentary lapse in judgment. It just irked him that Pastor Paul and the youth group was trying to impose their need to belatedly do something nice for Sarah on the cliff. The cliff was his spot, and Sarah's. If they wanted to remember her, why didn't they put the bench at the church?

In the end, he had given in on the bench because it wasn't worth the fight, especially with Pastor Paul threatening to ruin his credibility in the community. Luckily, his fear that the bench would attract more people to visit the cliff was unfounded. Once the bench was installed, everyone left him alone. It was rare that anyone came up here, until Janet.

Jonathon heard another noise from the back of the house. He pinpointed the location of the sound. It was time to swing into action. He crept along the side of the house, picking up a large stick that was leaning against the woodpile. To the casual observer, it looked like a walking stick. But Jonathon knew one end had been shaved to a sharp point. He would not go without a fight.

Janet thought that maybe Jonathon had not heard the window creak as she closed it back to where it was. But when she accidentally knocked over the screen as she was backing away from the window, she knew she was in trouble. She could run into the woods, but he would see her. No, she had to come up with something fast. Just as Jonathon rounded the corner of the house with the stick raised to strike, Janet knocked on the kitchen window as she peered inside, and called out "Professor Briggs? Jonathon? Are you home?"

Jonathon quickly dropped the stick to his side and answered. "Here I am. What are you doing back here?"

Janet screamed. She had expected him to enter the house, not come around the outside. She clasped her hands over her chest and turned toward him. "Oh wow, you really scared me. I thought you were inside."

"Most people go to the front door when calling on someone."

Janet hesitated for a moment then started talking very quickly. "Well, I did, but there was no answer. So, I thought you might be in the kitchen and not hear my knock, so I came around back. Then, I thought that maybe you were still asleep and I didn't want to wake you, so I tried to peek in through the kitchen window to see if I could see in before I knocked again and, when I did that, I knocked the screen down. Sorry, I can help you fix it. I hope it is not too early. I really didn't want to bother you."

Jonathon chuckled at himself and Janet. Now he could add paranoia to his list of preoccupations. He was glad that it was only Janet. In fact, he had cut his walk short this morning hoping to run into her at Sarah's bench. Now apparently, he had scared the bejeezers out of her.

The blood had drained from her face and she was rambling on. Thank God she said something before he came around the corner swinging. "Whoa, slow down. Sorry to startle you. I thought I had a raccoon or something on the prowl back here. Why don't we sit down for a moment and both catch our breath?"

They sat down on the edge of the back porch. Janet was glad for the pause. She needed to compose herself and figure out the rest of her story. Jonathon patted her hands as they lay on her lap. "So, my dear, what brings you here so early on a Sunday morning? My boyish charms or my Earl Grey tea?"

Janet looked up at Jonathon with a broad smile. She realized he was flirting with her and she relaxed. This would be her ticket out of her predicament. And, if truth be known, he was fun to flirt with.

Although she wasn't as physically attracted to him as Pastor Paul, Janet liked Jonathon. He was smart and witty, and had done thoughtful things for her since the first day they met. "Books," Janet replied, "Actually, I came for more books. But the other two would certainly be a welcome bonus."

They went inside the house and Jonathon turned on the tea kettle while Janet selected a book of poetry and essays by Thoreau. That was the first name Janet could remember from the Collection book of poems Jonathon gave her yesterday. While they were sipping their tea and chatting, Janet told Jonathon that she was interested in Thoreau's style and voice and wanted to see more of his work.

When Jonathon asked Janet if she wanted to take off her coat, Janet remembered the notebook and that it must be getting late. She looked at the clock on the wall. "No but thank you. I'm still a little chilly and I really should head out. Thanks again for the tea and the assistance. You are a very gracious host to a prowling raccoon!"

Jonathon smiled. He liked her sense of humor and enjoyed her company. "You don't have to rush off on my account."

"Oh, it's not because of you. I am supposed to be in church in less than an hour."

"Supposed to be in church? That doesn't sound like the talk of a true believer. Aren't you supposed to want to go to church or need to go to church or something?"

Janet giggled. "Ah, busted. You are perceptive. Let's just say that I'm giving it a trial run today, for a friend."

Jonathon walked Janet to the front door. He clasped his hands around hers as a good bye gesture. "I enjoyed the surprise visit. Come again anytime, but next time let's skip the "surprise" part. If I'm not at home, just wait for me here on the front porch. I'm never gone for long."

Janet blushed as she smiled at him, still a little embarrassed about being caught on the back porch. "Right, got it. Thanks again. I'll see you soon."

"I hope so."

Janet headed down the path back to her cottage. Jonathon watched her until she was no longer in sight. He whistled a tune as he tidied up the living room and carried the empty tea cups to the sink. He set them on the counter and headed to the shower. Halfway there he stopped whistling.

It dawned on him that something wasn't right in the kitchen. He went back to the sink and looked at what he thought he had seen. He shook his head in disbelief. There in the sink was a faint footprint from a woman's shoe. "My dear Ms. Reed," Jonathon said. "What have you been up to?"

CHAPTER 11

The church service had already begun by the time Janet got there. She slipped into a back pew. It felt good to sit down. She had been rushing around all morning. Janet had been tempted to stay at the cottage and read Sarah's notebook, but she didn't want to disappoint Paul. So, she stashed the notebook between her mattresses, jumped into the shower, changed and drove to church.

Paul nodded to her slightly when she came in. During his sermon, Janet felt that he was talking directly to her. She wondered if anyone else noticed. She looked around at the other parishioners. They were all paying rapt attention to Paul's words. Janet realized that they all felt that Pastor Paul was talking directly to them. They were drawn to his words, just as she was drawn to him. He does have a gift, Janet thought, feeling strangely proud.

After the service, Janet followed the crowd into the activities room in the church annex, where coffee and doughnuts were being served. She watched Paul as he entered the room, shaking hands and chatting with his flock. He glanced over at her and gave her a quick smile. She knew he would make his way toward her, but he had to go through the gauntlet of his faithful first. She could wait.

Janet grabbed some coffee and a doughnut. She was hungry after her morning's activities. When Paul finally approached her, he was accompanied by a generously proportioned woman in her late forties, who was holding on to his arm. Her clothes were dated but stylish, and she had an attractive face; although Janet thought she wore a little too much make-up.

"Good morning, Ms. Reed." Paul began.

"Good morning, Pastor Paul." Janet replied as nonchalantly as she could.

"Janet Reed, I would like you to meet Charlene Monroe, Sarah's mother. Charlene, this is the lady from Texas that I was telling you about, who was inspired by Sarah's memorial bench to do something similar for her son who recently passed away."

Janet set her coffee down on the table beside her and extended her hand to greet Charlene. "Very nice to meet you," Janet said.

Charlene took Janet's hand in hers. "Yes," she replied as she looked into Janet's eyes. The two women stood there silently, with hands clasped, for a moment. No other words needed to be said. They were initiated members of a special club. A club no one wanted to belong to.

Pastor Paul broke the silence, "Say, if you ladies would like to sit and chat in private, you're welcome to use my office. It's almost time for the 11:00 service so I won't need it anytime soon."

"Yes, that would be nice," Charlene said. She already felt a connection with Janet. She spoke directly to Janet. "I was thinking about having you over for some iced tea this afternoon at the nursing home, but we just found out the state regulators are coming tomorrow for a 'surprise' inspection and Ms. Massing has everyone running around like chickens with our heads cut off. So, it's not going to be our usual peaceful Sunday afternoon."

"Well, it was nice of you to think about me, anyway. Maybe we should take Pastor Paul up on his offer and chat for a few minutes now," Janet said.

Paul refilled their coffee cups and led them to his office and unlocked the door. "Make yourselves at home," he said as he ushered them inside. "I'll be back after the service." Paul closed the door behind him as he left. Janet and Charlene settled into the visitor chairs opposite Paul's desk. Janet spoke first.

"I really hope I'm not troubling you. I just think the memorial bench that you had done for Sarah was really touching."

"Well, I'll be honest, that bench was more the doing of the church. The kids, you know, of the youth group. They wanted to do something. Of course, they talked to me about it, but Pastor Paul did most of the work."

"Yes, he gave me a lot of information already. It will save me a lot of research and trouble when I go home and arrange for a bench for my son."

"What's your son's name?"

"Daniel."

"Daniel, that's a good biblical name, just like Sarah. I bet he was a sweet boy."

Janet choked up a little when Charlene mentioned her nickname for Daniel. "Yes, yes he was. That's what I used to call him sometimes, 'My Sweet Boy'."

Charlene reached over and held Janet's hand. "How long has it been?"

"Three months. And Sarah?"

"Just over five months. It gets a little easier, but it never goes away, you know, the feeling of loss."

"No, I don't guess that it will."

"How did it happen?"

Janet hated when people asked her that question and usually avoided answering it; but now, sitting here with Charlene holding her hand, it felt like a perfectly natural question. So Janet told the story about the day Daniel died, to someone she knew wouldn't judge, patronize, or pity her.

"It was track and field day at Daniel's school. He loved track and field day. I did too. The kids were always so full of energy and team spirit. Most of them were just happy to be spending the day outdoors running around and eating snocones or whatever other goodies the PTA was selling that year.

Daniel was in fifth grade, so it was the last track and field day for him at the school. He was particularly excited about his prospects of winning some races this year, since he had been doing some training and his father had promised to come and watch. His father is a very busy businessman and didn't always make it to Daniel's events.

The morning had been a great success. Daniel had won a handful of first and second place medals for various individual and team events. He was the most proud of the medal he got for tying Tony Gonzales for first place in the 400 meters sprint. Tony had won that event for the past two years.

I remember that it was the first thing that Daniel said to his Dad when he showed up that afternoon. Daniel was always so patient about his Dad's work schedule, much more so than I was. He would be disappointed when his Dad couldn't come, but he never got angry with him.

He was so excited that his father got there before the fifth-grade class 1600-meter relay. Daniel had just walked over to ask me if I'd seen his Dad, when Robert walked up to us. I'll never forget that conversation.

'Hey sport, looks like you got quite a collection of medals already. Hope I'm not too late to see you collect one more.' Robert said.

'Dad, you're not gonna believe it! I tied Tony for first in the 400 meters!'

'Of course I believe it. I knew your day was coming, what with the way you've been growing and doing some training. Just wish I could have seen it.'

'You still can. Tony and I are both going to be the anchor leg for our classes in the last relay of the day, the 1600-meter relay. It will be like a rematch.'

'Perfect, last race of day, rematch, you just go out there and give it your all. No holding back. I will be at the finish line, waiting to snap your picture when you cross ahead of Tony Gonzales.'

'You got it Dad.'

'Go get 'em, Tiger.'

They were both grinning and giving each other double thumbs up. Daniel started to run off to join his team mates and get ready for the race. They were up after the girls' relay. I shouted after him. 'Good luck, Daniel. Drink some water before the race.'

He yelled back without looking at me. 'Ok Mom. Love ya.'

That was the last thing he ever said to me. 'Ok Mom. Love ya.' 'Love ya' had been our goodbye to each other for years. I know he said it as an automatic reflex, but I will be forever thankful that we had that habit.

Robert and I made our way over to the track for the relay race. The girls' race was just finishing up. We stood by the starting line, which was also the finish line. There were four runners on each team. Each runner would run once around the track and hand off the baton to the next runner. The fourth runner was usually the strongest runner on the team and would be the one who raced for the finish line.

Daniel was huddled with his team mates doing their class cheer when we took our spot along the track. They broke and took their positions. Daniel looked over at us and gave us a wide grin and a quick wave. Robert gave him another thumbs up.

When the race began, Daniel started jumping up and down in place, watching as the first three runners sprinted around the track. I could tell he was nervous. The smile faded from his face as he anticipated the handoff from the third runner. There was probably only a ten-yard spread between the first and last of the four teams when the anchor men got their batons.

The big race was on. By the time they reached the first turn, Daniel and Tony had pulled away from the other two runners, with Tony holding a slight lead. They were neck in neck as they made the second turn and came down the home stretch. The whole crowd was cheering; some for Tony, some for Daniel. It was so exciting. With just twenty yards to go to the finish line, Daniel started to pull ahead. Tony accelerated and ran up right on Daniel's heels.

'He's going to trip him,' I remember saying to Robert.

'No, no, Daniel has a step on him. Watch, watch…. Come on Daniel. Finish strong!' Robert yelled as he aimed his camera at the finish line.

Daniel gave a final push and crossed the finish line three strides ahead of Tony. As he crossed the finish line, Daniel raised a fist in the air and looked over at his Dad. Robert was snapping pictures like crazy. Daniel was mobbed by his teammates. He was still trying to catch his breath, but he was grinning from ear to ear.

Daniel and his team mates started to walk over to get their medals when suddenly Daniel stopped. He was not smiling anymore, and the blood had drained from his face. 'Oh my God,' I screamed to Robert, as I pulled the camera away from his face. 'Something's wrong with Daniel!'

Daniel had already collapsed on the track by the time we got to him. Robert rolled him over and I felt his head. He was clammy. It didn't look like he was breathing. The P.E. teacher arrived right after we did and pushed me aside. She checked Daniel's pulse. 'Call 9-1-1,' she yelled. Robert already had his phone out and was dialing as she spoke. She began administering CPR. I knelt beside him on the other side and held his hand. I pleaded with him to wake up.

It took the ambulance six minutes to get there. It was the longest six minutes of my life. By the time they started applying the defibrillator, Daniel had been down for eight minutes. He never regained consciousness. He was declared dead at the scene."

Janet paused for a moment. Charlene just squeezed her hand. Tears were silently running down both of their faces. Janet reached over and got tissues from Pastor Paul's desk for both of them. She finished the story. Reciting the clinical cause of death helped her to maintain control of her emotions.

"The autopsy said that Daniel died from a condition called idiopathic myocardial hypertrophy with fibroelastosis of the left ventricle; an irregular heartbeat condition that he apparently had since birth. It's asymptomatic. People with this condition are at risk of sudden cardiac arrest at any time in their lives, especially when under extreme physical or emotional stress. We had no clue that he had that condition. He had always been a healthy boy."

"In a way, it was a blessing." This is not what Janet had expected Charlene to say.

"A blessing?"

"Not that he died. But if he had to die, it was perfect. Winning the race, fulfilling a dream with both his parents there with him, proud of him, adoring him, a hero to his class. That will always be his last memory of life on earth before he went to join our Lord in heaven. It's beautiful really."

Janet was astonished by Charlene's observation. She had never thought of it that way before. It put Daniel's death in a whole new light. These last three months she had been focused on her grief, her loss, the future Daniel lost. She envied Charlene's faith and perspective. Her instincts had been right about sharing the story with Charlene. She looked Charlene in the eyes and said. "Thank you, Charlene, thank you for that. It will help bring me some peace." Charlene started sobbing.

CHAPTER 12

Janet didn't quite know what to do. She didn't understand why Charlene would be sobbing after she thanked her for offering a positive perspective on Daniel's death. Had she been insensitive? Janet offered Charlene some more tissues and patted her hand.

"Excuse me, Janet. It's just that, I don't have peace. I wasn't there when my Sarah died. There are some things I will never know for sure."

Janet remembered the controversy Missy told her about surrounding Sarah's death. Yes, a suicide death of a child would be harder to handle. Janet remembered the notebook stuffed between her mattresses and felt a twinge of guilt. She was about to say something to Charlene about it, when Charlene continued. "I have a secret Janet, a secret nobody knows, and it may have got my baby girl killed."

Janet was momentarily speechless. What in the world could she mean? She decided to comfort and gently prod for more information at the same time; another skill from her former employment. "Charlene, certainly any secret from your past could not possibly have led to Sarah's death."

"Janet, I trust you. I can't carry this burden alone any more. Pastor Paul said you used to be a reporter."

"Yes, that's right."

"Well, can I tell you something and then ask you to find out if it's true?"

Janet's reporting instincts were now on high alert. "Sure, Charlene. I'll help you if I can."

"I think I know who killed my daughter."

Janet was on the edge of her chair, looking Charlene straight in the eyes. "Go on."

"What I'm going to tell you, I haven't told to nobody. You have to promise to keep it secret."

"I promise."

"My last name is not Monroe; neither is Sarah's. And we're not really from Shreveport, like I told all of the nice folks here." Janet let Charlene take a breath and said nothing. She knew there was time for silence in interviews and this was one of them.

Charlene continued her story. "We're from New Orleans. We left when Katrina hit. But there is more. A few days before the hurricane, I came home early from working at the hospital 'cuz I was getting a migraine.

When I got home, I heard Sarah crying and saying, 'No Papa, no.' Papa is what she called my husband. He was the only father Sarah had ever known. I married him when Sarah was eight. He was a good man then, but a few years ago, he lost his job and then he started drinking and gambling.

We started fighting more. He roughed me up a couple of times when he was drunk, but he never touched Sarah. And he would always be so sweet to me for days after he hit me. I know it was just the booze. He never meant to hurt me. I swear if I'd known he'd hurt her…," Charlene put a tissue to her eyes and wiped her tears.

"It's okay, Charlene, tell me what happened."

"I came into the house and they didn't hear me. I went to where the noises were coming from, to Sarah's room. He was drunk. I could smell it from the doorway. When I went in the room, I saw him in the bed on top of her. His pants were down, and her skirt was pulled up around her waist. I looked at Sarah. She had tears streaming down her face.

I guess I went a little crazy and started screaming at him and hitting him with my purse. I wish I'd had a baseball bat. He stood up and swung at me. Hit me square in the jaw, sent me flying backwards.

Sarah crawled out of the bed and tried to hide in the corner. I got back up and went at him with my fists a flying. I'd never hit him before and he was plenty pissed off about it. It was the worst fight we ever had. All of us were screaming and hitting at each other, except Sarah. She just sat there huddled in the corner.

I guess the neighbors called the cops, because they showed up a little while later and broke up the fight. They hauled him off to jail for drunk and disorderly and for assaulting me. We didn't say anything about Sarah. I needed some time to think about that. Didn't know the best thing to do."

"Oh Charlene, how horrid. Then what happened?"

"Well, the next day they said a hurricane was coming, that we were supposed to evacuate the city. We lived in Holy Cross, just below the Ninth Ward. I was scared to stay and scared to leave. The news reports said that we could die if we didn't evacuate, but I knew he would be mad if he came home and we were gone. I spent the whole day trying to figure out what to do.

When I woke up, I called the Orleans Parish jail to see if they knew when he would be released. They don't keep you very long for drinking and fighting in New Orleans. Anyway, they told me that they were in emergency lock down because of the storm. Anyone that was in now would have to stay there until after the storm passed.

Lord help me, but at that moment, I saw a chance for a better life for me and Sarah. I knew he kept some gambling money in a box under a board in his closet. It wasn't a fortune, but we could get by on it for a little while. I took it, and Sarah and I left the house to get on an evacuation bus. I told Sarah that we never wanted him to find us; that we wanted him to think that we died in the hurricane. So, we were going to change our last name and move far away.

We never found a bus to get on, but we followed some other folks to the Superdome. We were told that a shelter was set up inside and it was a safe place to ride out the storm. When we checked in, I put down our last name as Monroe because it was the first thing I thought of. I have an aunt with that last name. Then we found a place to sit by the concrete wall in the hallway and waited for the storm to hit."

"Oh Charlene, I can imagine how terrifying that must have been for you and Sarah."

"No one can imagine how terrible it was. The rain and the wind started pounding the building. Then, the top layer of the roof started peeling back. It sounded like an 18-wheeler had slammed on its brakes and was screeching out of control over our heads. I just sat huddled up with Sarah, shaking and praying.

Then, water started pouring onto the field through some holes in the roof. People started screaming and crying and running up to higher ground. Sarah and I just stayed put 'cuz we were already on the middle deck.

After the hurricane finally passed over us, people started cheering, but then the flooding started, I think they called it a storm surge, and we were all trapped. There was no air conditioning, so it got real hot. People was hungry and thirsty and there wasn't much food or water. People got frustrated, running around shouting and fighting. I didn't sleep for days. I felt like I had to guard Sarah and my money. I didn't know what was going to happen next.

Finally, they came and got us. We spent the next few days in another shelter in Reliant Stadium in Houston. All we did was watch the news reports on the hurricane damage and flooding. It was worse than I imagined. I knew our house was gone.

I was actually relieved 'cuz I thought my plan might work. He would think we were dead, his money and all our other belongings washed away. I didn't want to wait around for him to get out, so Sarah and I left the shelter and headed west.

I tried to be so careful not to leave tracks. I didn't take any FEMA money or nothing. I worked a few odd jobs as we traveled, and then in Phoenix, I paid a man to make me a fake social security card with Charlene Monroe on it, so I could get a better job. We finally ended up here when I found a job at the nursing home as a cook."

Janet let Charlene catch her breath. "Wow, Charlene, that's incredible! I admire your fortitude. But I don't see how that makes Sarah's death your fault? Do you think she was distraught over everything that happened?"

"No, I mean she was, when we first got here, but when she died, she seemed happier than I'd seen her in a while. The youth group and Pastor Paul had done wonders for her spirit. It took a little while, but she was finally becoming herself again."

Charlene leaned forward and grabbed Janet's arm with both her hands and pleaded. "Janet, please, I am so afraid that somehow he found us. Maybe it was a mistake to use my aunt's name; maybe he figured it out and he tracked us down here. I think he might have pushed her off that cliff to get back at me.

She wouldn't have jumped; I know that for sure. He might still be out there, waiting for a turn at me, after he lets me suffer enough. I don't know what happened to him after the hurricane. Please Janet, you're a reporter. Could you please help me find out what happened to him? If he died or were still in jail, I could have some peace. I could know that I didn't cause Sarah's death." Charlene started to cry again.

Janet rubbed Charlene's arm with her free hand. "Charlene," she said softly, "It's okay. You tried to protect Sarah. You could never be held accountable for what happened to her, even if it was your husband."

"But Janet, you understand, I have to know. I have to know the truth about what happened to Sarah."

Janet did understand. She would want to know too. And for the first time, Janet was thankful that she watched Daniel die. The horror of the moment was eclipsed by the peace of mind of knowing what happened; knowing that his last memories included her and Robert; and being able to hold his hand one last time. "Ok, Charlene. I'll see what I can find out. What's his name?"

"Dewayne. Dewayne Williams."

CHAPTER 13

Janet was alone in the office when Pastor Paul returned. Charlene left shortly after securing Janet's promise to try and locate her husband. She said she had to make sure the kitchen at the nursing home was spic 'n span for the regulators tomorrow. Janet thought she might be a little embarrassed since she left abruptly. It's hard to trust a stranger with a secret like that. But then, Janet mused, we're not really strangers, Charlene and me. We have the same scar on our hearts. We can trust each other. We both knew it from the moment we shook hands.

Janet's shoes were off, and her feet were resting on Charlene's empty chair when Paul came in and closed the door. He came over, lifted Janet's feet up and sat down underneath them. He began rubbing her feet.

"I saw Charlene leave a little while ago. I was hoping you would still be here. Did you have a nice chat?"

"Yes. Thank you for introducing her to me. I've never gotten so much from a single conversation before."

"Good. I was hoping you two would bond. It helps to share with someone who can relate to you."

Janet sighed. The foot massage felt great. All the events of the morning, which had been swirling around in her head since Charlene left, were quickly melting away in his hands. She didn't want to think about any of them, right now, not the notebook, not Daniel's death, not Charlene's secret. She just wanted to be here, in this moment, with Paul. Janet smiled at Paul.

"You know, this massage business of yours is habit forming. If you keep it up, I'm going to have to visit you everyday."

"I'm counting on it." Paul flashed Janet a cocky smile.

There was a knock on the door. Janet quickly withdrew her feet and slipped on her sandals. Paul went to answer the door. It was Pastor Harrington, the senior pastor at the church. He spoke with Paul for a few minutes at the door. Paul ended the conversation by telling Pastor Harrington that he would join him in his office as soon as he finished talking with the new church visitor. Paul shut the door and turned back to Janet.

"Never a dull moment around here. I have to attend to some church business for a little while."

"It's time I got back anyway." Janet stood up and headed toward the door. "Thanks again, for everything." Janet lingered on that last word as she looked at Paul.

"Well, I was hoping to see you later. Are you free this afternoon?"

Janet did want to get back and look at Sarah's notebook, but she was not going to pass up a chance to spend some more time with Paul. "Sure, as long I'm back home by five." Robert would not be home until at least 5:30, she thought to herself.

"Great, do you like to hike?"

"Yes, I hike around the greenbelts in Austin all the time."

"How about I meet you at 2:00 at McNee Ranch State Park? It's right off Highway 1. We can hike the Montara Mountain trails."

"Mountain Trail! How big is this mountain? I'm used to hiking on flat creek areas."

"Luckily for you I know a short cut on the north slope of the mountain that let's us start halfway up from the summit. Get on Highway 1, heading north of Montara, then turn east onto Linda Mar, then right onto Adobe, and finally, left onto Higgins Way. It's a dead-end street. We can park and start from there."

"Okay, I think I can find that. See you soon."

The McNee Ranch State Park is a primitive scenic park, full of native plants and animals. The hiking paths consist of old fire roads that are perfect for hiking or biking. Janet and Paul arrived practically at the same time. Paul took her hand and led her to the trailhead. As they walked along, he told her the names of some of the plants and trees.

There was quite a variety, some eucalyptus trees, coyote brush, bush monkeyflower, California sagebrush, bush lupine, pampas grass, a few cypress trees and some Monterey pine. At one point Janet wanted to get a closer look at the orange blossoms of the monkeyflower, but Paul cautioned her to stay on the path since poison oak was also abundant on the sides of the road.

The final ascent to the peak was arduous, so there was no conversation. Neither of them seemed to mind. There is a primeval bonding that occurs between hikers during those voiceless times, sharing a physical quest surrounded by nature's splendor. It's almost mystical and they could both feel it.

The view from the top was breathtaking. To the east they could see rolling green hills, all of San Francisco Bay and Mount Diablo; to the west, Devil's slide and the Pacific Ocean. Paul put his arm around Janet's shoulders as they stood there, catching their breath, admiring the panorama.

"This is magnificent," Janet said.

"Yes, I thought you would like it. We have an excellent day; sometimes the fog can obscure the view."

They sat down on a rock facing east. The breeze from the ocean was picking up and felt a little chilly. Paul wrapped his arms around Janet. She didn't say she was cold and in fact had on a windbreaker, but he didn't care. He wanted to hold her. She snuggled in against his shoulder.

They sat that way for a while, looking out over the horizon, each waiting for the other to make a move. Paul sensed the time was right, and leaned back on the rock, pulling Janet on top of him. They kissed, a long slow deep kiss, followed by increasingly frantic kisses. Paul reached his hands inside Janet's jacket and felt under her shirt for her breasts. His hands were cool, and her nipples hardened quickly at his touch. As he gently squeezed them, she moaned softly and pressed her body against his pelvis. She could feel that he was hard.

Their kisses became more intense as Paul thrust his tongue deep into her mouth. A crackling noise in the brush behind them snapped them back to a seated position. They were breathing heavily as they turned to look to see who was coming. Paul laughed as a pair of brush rabbits came into the clearing. "Popular spot."

Janet pulled her shirt and jacket back down around her. The wind had turned from mild to brisk. Paul knew the moment had passed. This wasn't the safest place to go undetected either. They would both be jumpy now. It was time to head back down. "Shall we head back down to the cars?"

"Yes, it is really getting cold up here."

"Maybe we can find another place to warm up along the way." Paul squeezed Janet's hand. She smiled at him.

They headed down the path hand in hand. As they approached a fork in the road, they saw another hiker and released hands. They arrived at the fork at the same time as the other hiker. It was Professor Briggs.

They all traded greetings and chatted briefly about the weather and the views on the trail. They were artificially formal. The forced exchange of pleasantries, Janet knew was done for her sake. It was more than just awkward, she though; it was obvious that the two men disliked each other.

"Oh, by the way, Janet," Jonathon continued, using her first name for the first time in this conversation, "I found a gold earring in the kitchen this morning after you left. Did you lose yours?"

Janet hesitated. Her mind was whirling. Did she have on earrings this morning? Did she lose one? In the kitchen? She hadn't spent any time in the kitchen after she and Jonathon came inside. Did he notice that? Think, think, think. No, she didn't have earrings on this morning because she remembered putting on a pair of diamond studs after her shower this morning before church. She hadn't taken any off to put them on. She subconsciously felt her ears. The diamond studs were still on. She hadn't worn other earrings today.

"No, I don't think I had any earrings on this morning," Janet replied. "It must belong to one of your other female visitors."

Jonathon laughed out loud. Janet realized immediately she had chosen her words badly. She would have laughed too if Paul had not been present. She blushed and tried to explain. "Not that I'm implying that you have a lot of other female visitors. I mean, I don't know if you have any female visitors, except me. I mean, not that I am a female visitor in the sense of a 'female visitor'. What I mean is, whether you have other visitors or not, it's not my earring." This wasn't helping matters.

Jonathon was still laughing, and Paul was not laughing at all. "Okay, just asking." Jonathon said, finally rescuing her from herself. "Well, I guess I will continue on my walk. Have a good afternoon." Jonathon said to them both. Then he looked only at Janet and said. "I'll see you soon."

Jonathon was pleased with himself as he walked away from them. He had gotten the reaction he wanted from both of them. Janet's hesitation and bumbling speech confirmed his suspicion that she had been inside his house before he came home from his walk this morning. Paul didn't do a very good job at hiding his shock that Janet had been at his house earlier this morning either. Janet sounded like she was guilty about something too. Paul would, of course, assume the worst.

Jonathon chuckled to himself as he headed off down the trail. He bet their starry-eyed conversation took on a new twist after he left. When he saw the two of them together, he wanted Paul to know that there was more than one horse in this race. The thought of a competition with Pastor Paul in anything rejuvenated him. With Janet as the prize, it just sweetened the pot.

Maybe he should kick it up a notch. Maybe he should visit her tonight. He did still need to find out what she was looking for this morning. He could be charming and probing at the same time. That used to be his livelihood.

CHAPTER 14

On the way back to the cabin from the State Park, Janet stopped at the market to pick up a few steaks and some wine for dinner. Robert would want to celebrate. But her mind was not on Robert or his work. She kept thinking about the end of her hike with Paul. His mood changed after their encounter with Jonathon. He became quiet and serious. She explained that she visited Professor Briggs to borrow some poetry books to research poems for Daniel's bench.

Paul told her that he didn't think she should be going up to Professor Briggs house alone. He said Professor Briggs wasn't all he claimed to be, but he wouldn't elaborate on it. "It's best if you have as little to do with him as possible, just trust me on this. We have an excellent library in Half Moon Bay. You should go there for your research," was Paul's final comment on the subject.

They headed back to their cars shortly after that. He gave her a quick kiss and said he would call her tomorrow. Janet didn't really understand Paul's objection. She knew they had a controversy over Sarah's bench, but Janet thought Jonathon was a perfect gentleman whenever she was around him and she always had a good time in his company.

Janet decided that Paul might be a little jealous. She was actually pleased that he was jealous. It meant he really liked her. She also knew that jealousy often spurred men into action and she was ready for a little action.

When Robert arrived home, Janet was marinating the steaks and making a salad. He set his briefcase down, came into the kitchen and kissed her on the cheek.

"Mmm, that smells good. When's dinner?"

"Whenever you're ready to grill the steaks. I already turned on the grill."

Janet handed Robert a glass of cabernet. She was already sipping on one. Robert sat down at the kitchen counter. She filled a small bowl with peanuts and set it in front of him. She knew he would tell her about his latest conquest before grilling the steaks. She refilled her wine glass.

Robert reviewed the highlights and controversies of the weekend meeting. There was one board member who was adamantly against the merger at the beginning. He was lobbying hard to get the other board members to vote the deal down. He had a few directors feeling skeptical.

In the end, Robert was able to convince them all of the advantages the merger held for both the company and the directors as well. The vote for the merger had been unanimous. Robert poured another glass of wine and sipped it, savoring the moment. That was the part he liked best; when he turned the opposition into allies.

Janet congratulated him and told him how much she admired his accomplishments. And she really did. Robert was good at what he did and made a good living doing it. He was excellent at crunching numbers, gave powerful presentations, and relentlessly badgered any opposition until they saw the errors of their ways. Most of his meetings ended with a handshake and a promise of a golf game in the near future. Janet's only complaint was that it consumed him. He never had much left for her, or Daniel.

In fact, he had thrown himself into his work even more since Daniel's death. She understood why. She had been looking for something to engross her as well. Had she found it here? She thought of the notebook tucked under her mattress and Charlene's secret. She thought of Daniel's bench and Jonathon. She thought of Paul. She looked at Robert and felt sad. She was reaching out to everyone except her husband. She decided to try.

"I went to Jack and Missy's church this morning. I met Sarah's mother there."

"Sarah?"

"The girl the lighthouse bench is dedicated to."

"Oh, yes, that Sarah."

"We had a nice talk. She told me Daniel's death was a blessing...."

"A blessing?!"

"She wasn't talking about the fact that he died, but about the way he died."

"I suppose she told you he saw a bright light and heard heavenly music right before the angels lifted him up to heaven."

"No, it wasn't like that. It's just that, the things she said, the way she said them, made me feel better about that day. I just wanted to share that with you."

"That's what church people do Janet. They tell you things to either make you feel better or scare you. Either way, you are more likely to come back and bring your money. It's a business like everything else; keep the customer coming back, keep the customer paying."

This is what Robert did when he didn't want to talk about something, especially something that might require him to show some emotion. He put up walls with sarcasm and cynicism. Well, she wasn't going to let Robert's skepticism spoil her revelation. She would drop it, change the subject. He wouldn't notice that they never finished the conversation, or if he did, he'd never show it. Avoidance, avoidance of sexual intimacy, avoidance of sharing emotions, avoidance of any real conversation; they were both very good at it. It was a mainstay of their marriage.

"I went for a hike this afternoon up on Montara Mountain. There are some spectacular vistas from up there."

"Oh really, I'll have to go up there sometime while we're here."

Janet would keep the rest of her Montara Mountain experience to herself. She just brought it up as a private salvo at Robert, for shutting her up, for shutting her out.

Robert refilled his wine glass and went out to grill the steaks. Janet set the table on the deck and tossed the salad. They ate dinner with very little conversation, talking only about Robert's schedule the next week, with an occasional comment on the sunset or the tranquility of the ocean. After dinner, Robert turned on the television and flipped through the channels. Janet brought out the books she borrowed from Jonathon and showed them to Robert. She started looking through them as he watched TV.

Robert went to bed early. He said he'd had a long weekend and had to get up early and drive back into San Francisco tomorrow morning. Janet said she wanted to stay up and read for a bit. While Robert was in the bathroom, Janet took the blue notebook out from under the mattress and stuck it between the poetry books on the living room table. She would wait until Robert was asleep before she started reading it. She didn't want to explain what it was or how she got it.

After Robert was in bed, Janet opened the notebook with anticipation. She was anxious to find out why everyone was so curious about what it contained. She quickly leafed through some pages. It contained mostly poems that appeared to be written by Sarah and a few quoted passages from well-known poets Sarah must have admired.

She turned back to the front and started reading. Sarah's poems were dark and full of anger, teenage angst on steroids. Storm images abounded; internal conflict and external chaos intermingled. After what Charlene told her today, she understood why.

After reading several of Sarah's poems, Janet put the notebook down on her chest. Her eyes welled up with tears. She felt Sarah's horror and despair from both storms that besieged her last year in New Orleans. They stripped her of her innocence and took away the only home she had known. Janet decided to rest her eyes for a moment before reading any further. It had been a long day. She was fast asleep in minutes.

Jonathon had been sitting on the dunes at the edge of the row of beach cottages for some time. He had come down to see Janet. He was almost to the cottage when he saw the second car. He had forgotten about Robert. He didn't like to think of her as married. It wouldn't serve either of his purposes to show up now. Still, he wanted to wait until they settled into bed to have a quick look around before he hiked back up to his house. He saw the light go out in the bedroom a half hour ago, but there was still a light on in the living room. He decided to go have a closer look.

Sneaking up around the side of the house, he was able to get a good view into the living room window without being seen. Janet was asleep in the chair. Jonathon scanned the rest of the room. Robert was nowhere to be seen. He looked back at Janet. There were three books on the table beside her and one open across her chest.

Jonathon felt a pang of guilt about putting her on the spot this afternoon. She really was trying to find a fitting poem for her son's memorial. Jonathon looked at her face as she slept. She looked so peaceful. He wished he could caress her face. He glanced down at her body; he could study it more deliberately now, while she slept. He liked what he saw.

He peeked up to see which author she had been reading before she drifted off to sleep. He didn't see a title. He looked closer. No, it couldn't be. It was a blue notebook, Sarah's notebook. Janet had found Sarah's notebook! He thought it had been lost for good. He continued to underestimate her.

For some reason, knowing that Janet had somehow acquired the notebook made her even more attractive to him. He had to figure out how to get it back; destroy the evidence it contained. But he would have to be patient, make his move later, when he could approach Janet alone. From what Janet had told him earlier, it wouldn't be a lengthy wait. Robert never stayed home for very long. This next time, however, he wouldn't underestimate Janet.

CHAPTER 15

Robert left first thing in the morning. He said he probably would stay in San Francisco the next few days. He and Jack had a lot of planning to do. They would be working late into the night. Janet gave him the American Poet Collection to look over, in case he had some spare time at the hotel before he went to sleep. "I really do want your input on a poem for Daniel's bench," she told him. He said he would look at it if he had time and threw it in his briefcase as he went out the door.

Janet was already heading to the Half Moon Bay library when Paul called her.

"Good Morning. Hope I'm not waking you?"

"Actually, I'm up and already on my way to the library to do some research." Janet didn't tell him she was doing some research for Charlene. It was best to let him think it was poetry for Daniel.

"Very industrious of you. Glad you took my advice about the library."

"Well, you do seem to have a good head on your shoulders," Janet said teasingly. She wished he could see her smiling through the phone.

"Oh, so I 'm just a pretty face to you," he joked back. Paul was also stalling. He wanted to ask her something, but he was a little nervous about it. This was unusual for him. He had slept with plenty of other women. Somehow, with Janet, it was different. He decided to stall a little longer; the fact that she was married did complicate matters. "Listen Janet, could you stop by my office after you're finished at the library. I want to ask you something."

"Why don't you ask me now?"

"Just thought it would be better to ask you in person."

"Are you trying to lure me to your office for another massage?"

"I can't pull anything over on you, can I?"

"Nope, that's why I get up early in the morning. I should be done by 2:00 or so. Will that work for you?"

"That'll be great. See you then."

The library at Half Moon Bay is housed in a 30-year-old building and is bursting at the seams. Janet grabbed one of the last public computers available. She put her pad of paper and Sarah's notebook down beside the computer and logged on. She figured she could keep reading through the notebook while she waited for her internet searches to download. She knew from experience that some public libraries had very slow connections. Motherhood had made her a great multitasker.

Janet started with the obvious search and googled 'Dewayne Williams New Orleans Parish Prison'. Nothing relevant came up.

She searched the parish court's website to see if there was a record of his case being tried after September 2005. It was another dead-end.

Apparently, the government entities in New Orleans still had not fully recovered all their records and online searching was limited. Janet decided this was going to be the case for all local records, and that her best bet was to research news stories about what happened at the jail just before, during and after Hurricane Katrina hit.

She input "Orleans Parish Prison" and "Katrina". Jackpot! She started clicking on the sites, gleaning whatever information she could out of each one, to try and figure out what happened to the inmates kept there during the hurricane. The more she read, the more she wanted to read. There were some conflicting reports, but in the end, she decided what happened in that prison was appalling.

The Orleans Parish Prison is not really a prison, but one of the largest county jails in the country. At any given time before Katrina struck, it held 6,000 to 7,500 inmates. By most accounts, on the morning Katrina made landfall, there were close to 6,500 inmates at the prison. Some were there serving sentences for misdemeanors or parole violations, and some were federal detainees housed at the prison under a contract with the U.S. Marshal's Service. Most had been arrested for offenses like criminal trespass, public drunkenness or disorderly conduct and were waiting to be brought before a judge for a trial. Many would have been released by the judge with just pretrial time served. That all changed when Katrina smashed into the city.

There was one news station report of a riot at the prison. But all other accounts told a different story. Human Rights Watch put out a press release one month after Katrina that told of some of the atrocities the inmates endured. Stories were told of guards abandoning the prison, with prisoners still locked in their cells, as generators failed, and flood waters started to rise. Many stood in feces filled water up to their necks before being rescued three days later.

In one facility, some inmates were locked in the gymnasium without food or water for two days. As flood waters rose around them, they heard the screams of prisoners still locked in their cells below them. Some prisoners told of bodies floating by. When the water floated them up to the windows in the gymnasium, some of the trapped prisoners managed to break out and swim to safety. Others set shirts on fire and hung them through the bars over the windows to signal for help.

A few of the prisoners interviewed who broke out of the prison said they turned themselves into the authorities right away so they could be evacuated out of the city. One month after Katrina, by the best count of Human Rights Watch, 517 prisoners were still unaccounted for.

The Sheriff for the parish said that all prisoners were evacuated from the prison within three days after the storm. All were transferred to other prisons and jails in Louisiana. Despite prisoner reports of dead bodies in the flood water, the coroner said that no one died in the prison.

A recent American Civil Liberties Union report that was just released this August, almost one year after the hurricane, stated that the prisoners in the Orleans Parish Prison "suffered some of the worst horrors of Hurricane Katrina." The ACLU demanded an investigation by the Department of Justice.

Janet found a site that described the efforts of a coalition of Louisiana attorney groups to locate all displaced inmates and work toward their release, especially those whose sentences had expired or who were being held only on misdemeanor charges. With over 8,000 displaced prisoners, this was a daunting task. Janet wondered how many they had secured releases for already and if Dewayne was one.

There was also a listing by the Department of Corrections that gave a hotline number for family members to locate which prison their loved ones were being held in. This information would only be given to immediate family members. No other information would be disclosed, including case status and scheduled release date. Given the amount of time that had expired, Janet wasn't sure the hotline would still be operating but she jotted down the number.

The librarian approached Janet and indicated that her 90 minutes were up and that there were other people waiting. Janet signed off and immediately put her name on the waiting list to get another turn at the computers. She found a chair over in the corner and sat down to wait. She flipped open her cell phone and dialed the hotline number. She knew it was a long shot. A recorded message came on. The hotline had been disconnected.

Janet sank back in her chair. Based on what she'd read so far, she realized that finding information on Dewayne Williams was going to be next to impossible. She didn't want to disappoint Charlene. There had to be another way to figure out what really happened to Sarah.

Janet thought of her friend Carlos Sanchez and wondered if he could find out some information for her. He was a crime reporter at the Austin American Statesman. He had some connections in law enforcement. Maybe he could find out something for her. She knew he would be discreet. She would have to get more background information first.

She dialed information to get the phone number for Cresthaven Nursing Home and called Charlene. Janet explained what she had found so far and asked her to pull together whatever personal information she could about Dewayne's birth date, social security number, last known address, and a picture if she had one. Charlene said she would see what she had. Janet told her she would be by around 1:15 to pick up whatever she came up with.

Janet looked over at the bank of computers. They were still full. She picked up Sarah's notebook and started skimming through it. There were more angry poems, and some poems with a lonely tone. Ocean analogies became more prominent. About halfway through the notebook, Janet noticed a distinct change in Sarah's writing. She scanned the poems, highlighting various stanzas in her mind as she read.

"I can count the hours that I've sat here,

Waiting, with bated breath, hoping."

"Oh, let me succumb to my desires."

"True love is supposed to be like this,

Jumping heart and soul with no net.

I trust you with myself completely."

"I am afloat on the ocean blue coolness of your eyes,

Basking in the afterglow of your touch.

Gently rocked by the rhythm of your heart."

It was clear to Janet that, not only had Sarah fallen in love with someone, but there was a good chance she had sex with him. No one she had talked to about Sarah had ever mentioned a love interest. No one else knew, Janet concluded. Sarah had a secret lover. This could put a new twist on what happened to her. Was she jilted by her secret lover? Would that have been the last straw in her sad year, distressing her so much that she would commit suicide?

Janet remembered that Missy mentioned the notebook because the authorities were looking for a suicide note. Janet continued looking through the notebook. There was nothing in the back pages of the notebook except for a few more doodles, and an untitled poem. No suicide note. She was glad, for Charlene's sake. Janet read the untitled poem.

"He doesn't know I know,

It slipped out in our chat.

The kindly old professor

And the literary brat.

He challenged me with Chaucer,

I countered with Millet.

And then I heard him say something

He didn't mean to say.

He called us kindred spirits,

Coming here to start anew.

Him from the east, me from the south,

But that didn't ring quite true.

He knew too much about the storm,

I told him I had seen.

Small details of the horrors known

By just those who had been."

Was Sarah referring to Jonathon? She was home schooled. What other professors could she know? It had to be Jonathon. He had told Janet in the lighthouse the other day that he had a chat with Sarah about poetry and other things. Janet read the poem again.

Sarah thought he had a secret, something he didn't want anyone else to know. She didn't believe he was from the east. She thought he witnessed Hurricane Katrina in person. That would mean he was from New Orleans, or at least was there during the storm. What was it Paul said yesterday? "He's not who he claims to be. Stay away from him." Janet had a new focus for her next internet search.

She closed the notebook and went to see how much longer she had to wait for another turn at the computers. The librarian said that she was next, and that computer number three had just opened up. Janet quickly logged in and searched for "Professor Jonathon Briggs". She was surprised by the number of sites that came up.

Jonathon Briggs was indeed an English professor who specialized in poetry. Some of the credentials she found for him included tenures at several schools, including Mississippi State University and a preparatory school near Boston. She kept searching. She hadn't found anything yet that conflicted with what Jonathon had told her. She knew he had mentioned Mississippi State. She thought he said he graduated from there, but she could be mistaken.

Then she saw it, an obituary that had been placed in the New Orleans Times Picayune in August 2005. Jonathon Briggs, beloved son of Alma Briggs of New Orleans Parish, died in a car crash in Boston. The article listed some of his career accomplishments, which corresponded to the information she found on the other sites. No other family was listed. There was a picture of Professor Briggs included with the article. Janet stared at the screen in disbelief. It was not the face of the Professor Briggs she knew. Janet printed the article, stuck it in the back of Sarah's notebook and left the library.

CHAPTER 16

When Janet walked into the lobby of the nursing home, she could sense the tension. The receptionist asked if she could help her and Janet told her she was there to see Charlene. She asked Janet to sign in the log book and called Charlene.

When Janet signed in, she remembered the reason everyone was a little edgy. The two previous entrants on the log were Matt Worley and Susan Cheng, both with the California Department of Social Services, Community Care Licensing Division. "She'll be right here. Please have a seat in the lobby," the receptionist said.

When Janet spotted Charlene coming down the hall, she stood up to greet her. Charlene had on an apron and a hairnet. She must have come straight from the kitchen. The women gave each other a quick hug and sat back down on the couch in the lobby.

"I'm sorry, Charlene, I forgot that the inspection was today. Did you have any time to get together the information I asked you for?"

Charlene reached into her apron pocket and pulled out a few scraps of paper and handed them to Janet. "Actually, since the regulators are here today, I had to take a break this morning, so I went back to my room and found what I could. I wrote down his birth date, address and what I think his social security number was. It used to be our ID number for our health insurance before he lost his job. I think I remembered it right."

"Great, that will help me a lot. Any pictures?"

Charlene reluctantly pulled a small picture out of her pocket and looked down at her lap. The picture had obviously been cut out of a larger wedding photo. "I don't know why I kept this," Charlene started to explain.

Janet laid her hand over Charlene's hand holding the picture. "No need to explain, Charlene, I understand. All marriages have good and bad. Sometimes, even when the bad gets out of control, it's hard to let go of the dream that it will all be good again."

Janet thought of her marriage. She had been holding on to that same dream for years now, the dream that someday it will get better. It was all that kept her with Robert, especially now that Daniel was gone. Not that her marriage was as bad as Charlene's appeared to have become. There was no violence, no gambling, no money problems. Heck, they rarely even had an argument. There was just a whole lot of nothing.

Charlene looked up at Janet and gave her a thankful look. "Okay, thank you Janet, for doing this for me. I better get back to the kitchen now."

As Charlene was leaving, Janet had another thought, "Charlene, do you happen to have a copy of Sarah's autopsy?"

"No, why?"

"I don't know, I just thought maybe it might give some clue as to what actually happened. It's something my editor always told me to check when investigating someone's death."

"Well, I never got a copy. People from the coroner's office kept asking me questions that made me think they were saying that Sarah killed herself. I told them she would never kill herself. If she committed suicide, she wouldn't go to heaven.

It was very upsetting to me. Pastor Paul told me not to worry, he would handle everything. He told me that the autopsy listed the cause of death as head trauma from falling off the cliff. He said they didn't list suicide on it. That was enough for me. Does that help you?"

Janet could see that she had upset Charlene. She decided not to mention anything about what she had read in Sarah's notebook yet. "Yes, Charlene, that's all I really needed to know. Like I said, I really wasn't sure what it could tell me."

The women hugged again and parted company. Charlene went back to her kitchen inspection and Janet off to meet with Pastor Paul. This morning he said he wanted to ask her something. She now had a few questions for him as well. But, how was she going to ask them without revealing Charlene's secret?

CHAPTER 17

Janet sat in the church parking lot, scrolling through the contact list on her cell phone until she found Carlos Sanchez. She dialed the number. She was still trying to figure out exactly what she was going to say when he picked up the phone.

"Hi Carlos, this is Janet Reed. Are you busy?"

"You know I'm never too busy for you, darlin'. How are you?"

Many of her former colleagues came to Daniel's funeral. A few, like herself, were embarrassed that they had let so much time slip by without any contact and they promised to stay in better touch after the funeral. Carlos was one of them.

"I'm fine. I'm in California right now. I came here with Robert on a business trip. Anyway, I have a little time on my hands, so I am working on a freelance story."

"That's great. Are you thinking about getting back into the biz? I just told Tom the other day that he should try and lure you back here."

"I don't know. I thought I would try my hand at one story first and see how it goes."

"What's it about?" Carlos asked.

"It's a piece on what happened in the New Orleans Parish prison during and after Katrina. I've read a few reports about it online, but I think a lot more has gone on then has been revealed. I met some Katrina refugees in Austin who had relatives there and they told some shocking stories."

Janet hated lying to Carlos, but she didn't want to betray Charlene's confidences. Besides, if Dewayne was out and didn't know where Charlene was, she didn't want to somehow lead him here.

"Wow sounds interesting. How can I help?"

"Well, I'm trying to track down what happened to one of the inmates. You know, trying to add some personal interest to the piece. Anyway, his aunt gave me his name, social, birth date and a picture, but I haven't had any luck locating where he was taken after Katrina. I thought you might be able to use your connections to help me out."

"I'll see what I can do. Why don't you fax me over what you have? I know someone over in the U.S. Marshal's Service in the Oklahoma District. Maybe he can find out something for us from a counterpart in Louisiana."

"Great. Thanks a lot, Carlos. Oh, and Carlos, I'm trying to keep this project quiet for now; you know, hoping to turn up some new information or a new angle."

"Gotcha, going for an expose piece. I remember you were good at those. No problem. I won't talk about it."

"You're the best."

"Just like you, Baby, just like you."

Janet smiled, remembering her days working with Carlos. They broke several key news stories together. It was a rocky partnership at first. They had different investigative styles, but soon found that those differences complemented each other. They became fast friends and each other's biggest fan.

Janet wrote down his fax number and told him she'd fax the information as soon as she found a fax machine. She promised to have lunch with him when she got back to Austin, and then hung up the phone and went inside the church.

Paul was working on papers at his desk when Janet arrived at his office. She stood in the doorway and watched him work for a moment before he realized she was there.

"Ah, there you are," Paul said as he walked over to Janet. "I have some good news." He had already decided following his telephone conversation with her this morning that the direct approach would be best. No use beating around the bush.

Paul gave Janet a quick hug, closed his door and escorted her over to the visitor chairs. They sat down. Paul leaned forward in his chair toward Janet and took her hands in his. Janet wasn't quite sure what to make of his burst of enthusiasm.

"I just got Pastor Harrington to give me the next two days off, and I've planned a trip to a secluded camp ground I know of down the coast. It's beautiful this time of year. Interested?" Paul smiled and raised one eyebrow.

Janet got the message loud and clear. This was a trip for two, to a place where they would not be interrupted or discovered. It was their chance to consummate what they both had been yearning for.

Yet, it seemed so premeditated. She would be going on a trip with another man, knowing she was going to cheat on Robert. It would have been easier if she had just let it happen the other night, after she had been drinking. At least she could use that as an excuse, if she regretted it or felt guilty.

What if she didn't regret it? What if she could find more joy in her life with Paul? She would never know if she didn't try. Robert wouldn't have to know for now. He wouldn't even be home until Wednesday night. Would he even care if he did find out? For all Janet knew, Robert had affairs on the road all the time. He certainly had plenty of opportunities.

Janet laughed at herself at that thought. She knew in her heart that he had not cheated on her; cheated her out of some passion and joy in her life, yes, but slept with another woman, no. His mistress was his work. Still, she wanted some of that passion and joy back, even if it was only for a few days.

Paul could see the wheels of rationalization spinning inside Janet's head. He remained quiet for another moment, hoping she would come to the same conclusion that he had. They wanted to be together. They needed to be together. If two days were all they were going to have, then they should make the most of it. Carpe Diem.

Paul squeezed Janet's hands. It was time to prod for an answer. "You won't have to do a thing, except pack a few clothes. I have all the equipment and will pick up any supplies that we'll need. Janet, I want to spend some time really getting to know you. I can't deny this connection that I feel with you. I know you feel it too." Then Paul broke into a mischievous grin and added, "And I promise to give you a massage el fresco."

Janet laughed. She had no defense against his disarming grin. "No fair, you know my Achilles heel. Heck, you created my Achilles heel!" She stopped laughing and looked into Paul's eyes and said softly, "Yes, yes. I will go with you."

"Terrific. You won't regret it. I promise. I'll pick you up tomorrow morning, say around 9?"

"That sounds perfect. I just have to be back before 5 on Wednesday."

"No problem."

They both knew the reason for the deadline, so no elaboration was necessary. They both also understood that this obscure reference would be the only mention of Robert between them during the next two days. They stood up and Paul gave her a hug and a kiss on the forehead. "I can't wait for tomorrow." He looked at the clock on the wall. "I hate to rush you off, but I have a meeting to go to and then paperwork to finish up before I can leave on the trip."

Janet remembered she wanted to ask Paul several questions about Sarah and Jonathon Briggs. It didn't seem as important now. Besides, she could ask him during the next few days. She still needed a fax machine though. "Do you know anywhere nearby that has a fax machine I can use? I need to send some information to a friend."

"I have one here in my office. It's behind my desk on that cabinet. You're welcome to use it if you want."

"That would be great. It's only a few pages. I'd be happy to pay for any charges."

"Don't be silly. It's no problem. Do you have the papers with you? I can send them for you now."

"Actually, they're in the car. I was going to stop at some place on the way home."

"Well, I have to head out to my meeting. Why don't you just go get your papers, sit at my desk and use my fax. It'll make me happy to come back and sit in my chair knowing it was warmed by your luscious bottom. Just close the door behind you when you leave."

"Ok, you've got a deal. Thanks."

Just as Paul was heading out, Janet thought of one other question. "Oh Paul, do you have a copy of Sarah's autopsy?"

Paul looked puzzled. "That's an odd question."

"Charlene told me she never got one and that you dealt with the coroner's office for her," Janet started to explain. She knew she needed a better explanation for why she wanted to see it, but she didn't want to give away Charlene's secret. Once again, Janet lied to protect Charlene.

"When Charlene and I were talking on Sunday, I told her the story of how Daniel died, but when it came to the cause of death, I recited the clinical findings from the autopsy. I told her it helped me control my emotions better. She said maybe she should get a copy of Sarah's autopsy to help her with that. I guess just being in your office again made me think of it. Just thought, if you did, I could bring her a copy."

Paul shook his head and relaxed. "I keep forgetting how women's minds run many trains on different tracks at the same time. I don't think I got a copy, but if I did, it would be in that file I showed you the other night. I'll leave it on my desk for you."

He walked over to his desk, unlocked his file drawer and tossed the file on the desk. He came over and gave Janet a quick kiss. "Now go on and get your papers. I really must go. Make yourself at home here. I'll call you tonight."

CHAPTER 18

Janet went out to her car and retrieved the information Charlene gave her. She came back in and sat down at Paul's desk. She thought about his comment about her bottom and beamed. She was getting excited about the camping trip. She wanted to finish up her promised work, head home and figure out what to pack.

Janet found a piece of paper and wrote a cover sheet to Carlos. "Carlos, I am sending the information we talked about on the next page. Name, social, picture, etc. are attached. He was in New Orleans Parish Prison when Katrina hit. Anything you can find would be great. Call me on my cell if you do. Thanks a bunch. See you next week! Janet."

On a second sheet of paper, Janet transcribed Dewayne Williams' personal information and taped his picture below that. She put both pages in the fax machine and hit 'send'. Carlos's fax machine was busy. It usually was. She would have to keep resending until she got through. She set Paul's machine to automatically resend every two minutes and turned to the file on the desk.

Janet flipped through the file, looking for an autopsy, but mostly she daydreamed about last Saturday night with Paul. She liked sitting in his chair. His scent still lingered in the air. She absentmindedly fondled his pen with her left hand. She got to the end of the file without finding an autopsy. She decided to put the file away for him, so his desk would be clean when he returned.

She opened the file drawer she saw him take it out of. She seemed to recall it came from the back. As Janet looked for a space at the rear of the drawer to put the memorial bench file, she spotted another file; one entitled "Jonathon Briggs." She stuffed the memorial bench file in the drawer and pulled out the Briggs file.

Eager to find out more about the imposter professor, Janet scrutinized the contents of the file. She was disappointed. Paul's file didn't contain anything she didn't already know. It was full of articles about who the real Jonathon Briggs was. It even contained an obituary from a Boston paper, along with a picture. Maybe that's why Paul didn't want to elaborate. He didn't know who our local Professor Briggs was, just who he wasn't.

Janet concluded that she knew more about who Professor Briggs was than Paul did, thanks to Sarah's poem and the obituary she found in the Picayune. She knew he had been in New Orleans around the time Katrina hit. He must have seen the obituary and decided it was a safe identity to assume, especially in California where it was unlikely anyone knew the real Jonathon Briggs.

At the back of Paul's file were several pictures of the fake Professor Briggs. They were unposed and looked like they were taken from a distance and blown up. Obviously, Paul, or someone, had taken these photos without his knowledge.

The fax machine finally beeped, indicating that her papers were being sent to Carlos. Janet had a flash. She grabbed one of the photos from the Briggs file and taped it to a piece of paper. She scribbled a quick note on the bottom. "Carlos - Another one - in N.O. during Katrina. Just have picture. Do what you can. XO, J." Janet finished her note and slipped the page into the fax machine just in time for it to go with her original message. She collected up her papers, put the Briggs file back where she found it, and left Paul's office.

On the way back to the cottage, Janet passed a county building. She noticed that "County Coroner" was listed on the marquee. She pulled into the parking lot. From her years as a reporter, Janet knew that the coroner's office would not just hand over an autopsy to anyone. She could get some information by filing a public information request, but that would take too much time. As a family member, Charlene could get a copy, but it was obvious that Charlene did not want to deal with the coroner's office and was not really that interested in getting a copy of the autopsy.

Janet's curiosity was piqued. No one seemed to have a copy of the autopsy. No one had studied it. She knew from previous experience that a lot of information about the circumstances surrounding a person's death could be gleaned from an autopsy; things, that on the surface, might not seem relevant. If she were going to help Charlene find out the true cause of Sarah's death, she needed to see a copy of that autopsy. There had to be a way for her to get it, quickly.

Janet thought again about calling Charlene, but then remembered that the regulators were still at the nursing home. That gave Janet, another idea; state government officials usually trump county government officials. What was the name she saw in the logbook? Cheng, Susan Cheng. It was worth a try.

Janet called information and got the number for the coroner's office. She dialed the number. Janet tried to disguise her voice and use a California accent. This was difficult since Janet wasn't quite sure what a California accent sounded like. To someone used to a Texas accent, a California accent sounded like a lack of any accent at all. She decided to mimic Missy.

"Hello, this is Susan Cheng, with the Community Care Licensing Division of the California Department of Social Services. May I have your records department, please?"

"I can help you with that," the clerk responded.

"Okay, good. We are inspecting the Cresthaven Nursing Home today and the autopsy records for residents at the home who died this past year are incomplete. I was wondering if I could get a copy of the missing records from you this afternoon."

"I guess that's possible, how many records are missing?"

"Just one actually, they're missing the autopsy for Sarah Monroe."

"Wasn't she the teenage girl that fell off the cliff? Why would that nursing home need a record of that?"

"Yes, that's the one, and that's what the nursing home thought too. But she did die while she was a resident of the nursing home, and technically, under our regulations, they must have a copy of her autopsy on file."

"Okay, I can make a copy of that for you. Do you want me to mail it to you, or to the nursing home?"

"I tell you what, we're trying to wrap up our inspection here today. I'll have Betsy Massing send someone over to pick it up this afternoon. When do you think it will be ready?"

"I can do it right away. I'll have it at the front desk in about 20 minutes."

"Terrific. I really appreciate your help with this. Someone will be around to pick it up shortly."

Janet spent the next 20 minutes poking around a few gift shops on Main Street. She picked up some lavender scented massage oil. After all, she knew a few massage techniques herself.

The coroner's office was in the back corner of the county building. Janet walked down a poorly lit corridor with a dated carpet until she reached the entrance. She paused for a moment before entering. She didn't want to appear too anxious.

When she stepped inside, Janet saw a young woman at the front desk. She was talking on the phone. Janet waited patiently while she finished her call.

"Can I help you?"

"Yes, Betsy Massing sent me over to pick up an autopsy report for the regulators."

"Here you go." The young woman handed Janet a sealed envelope.

"Thanks a lot." Janet said as she took the envelope and left the office.

Once inside her car, Janet looked around to make sure no one was watching her. Of course, no one was, but obtaining documents through deception always made her a little nervous. She opened the envelope and read the report. Time of death was estimated to be approximately 5:00 pm. The cause of death was listed as "blunt force trauma to the head".

The report went on to say that the injury was consistent with falling off a cliff and hitting the rocks below. Janet looked at the other medical notes made by the coroner. No drugs or alcohol were found in her system. She had multiple fractures and contusions that appear to have occurred subsequent to the head trauma. It was noted that this was consistent with being tossed against the rocks by the tide for hours.

A final paragraph noted that the subject had elevated levels of the hormone HCG in her blood and traces of placenta tissue were found in her uterus. Conclusion, subject most likely had a spontaneous abortion after the fall off the cliff; estimated gestation period was four weeks. Janet whistled under her breath and glanced over at Sarah's notebook. Her instincts about Sarah's later poems had been correct. Not only had Sarah had sex, she was pregnant when she died.

CHAPTER 19

Robert finished his scotch at the bar of the Seaside Inn. The bar was empty, except for the bartender and a young business man sitting at the other end at the bar. There were no good prospects tonight. There rarely were on Monday nights. Robert paid his bar tab and went to check in. He wasn't too disappointed. He was tired after meeting all day with Jack Allen. Besides, he would stay here again tomorrow night. There were usually more couples in a bar on a Tuesday.

Robert went inside his room, tossed his briefcase on the bed and stripped down to his boxers. He sat on the bed and opened the briefcase, thinking that he might as well recheck the last set of numbers he gave Jack before tomorrow morning. The poetry book that Janet gave him that morning caught his eye. He picked it up and set it on his lap.

Robert felt badly about cutting Janet off last night when she tried to talk about Daniel's death. He knew he should talk about his feelings and his grief, but he couldn't, especially with Janet. Yes, they both lost a son, and they both missed him terribly. But Robert felt a greater loss. He didn't just miss Daniel; he missed out. He missed out on a lot of little things and, if he were honest with himself, some big things too.

At least Janet had her memories of Daniel. He only had the memories of what he planned to do with Daniel. It's not the way he planned it. It just happened that way.

Janet was better with Daniel when he was young. She had more patience than he did, he'd be the first to admit that. So, he spent a lot of time working. It was not just for his career advancement, but for the whole family. He earned his stripes during those early years of working hard. He was just now getting to the place in his career where he could control his schedule more. He would have had more time for Daniel when Daniel needed him most, as a young man.

Robert had already planned a raft trip on the Colorado River through the middle of the Grand Canyon. It was going to be a guy's trip, just him and Daniel. He was waiting for Daniel to turn 12. He wanted Daniel to be strong enough to handle the rigors of class three and four rapids.

Football season was just around the corner. It would have been Daniel's first year on the middle school team. Robert had promised Daniel that he would schedule his out-of-town meetings around game days. He had encouraged Daniel to try to get faster. He thought his son would make a great receiver.

He had dreamed of the years he would spend going to Daniel's high school football games. He would keep his own set of stats on Daniel's performance and in his junior year shoot video at the games to make a highlight tape to send to college recruiters.

The part he used to think about the most though was how it would be after the games, when Daniel would come home and sit with Robert on the back porch. They would rehash the high points and low points of the game. And, Robert would share a few of his high school football stories with his son. But, win or lose, good performance or mediocre, Robert would have always told Daniel how proud he was of him.

Robert reached over for his wallet lying on the nightstand and pulled out a picture. It was the picture of Daniel as he crossed the finish line, the day he died. His fist was raised in victory. He had a broad grin across his face and Daniel was looking directly into the camera, directly at Robert, in his moment of glory. Robert had been so proud, and so glad that he had been there to witness Daniel's triumph.

Tears welled up in Robert's eyes as he gazed at the picture. Looking at it was always bittersweet for Robert. Often, after Daniel died, Robert wondered if Daniel had pushed himself beyond his limits to impress him. If he had shown up for Daniel's activities more often, maybe this wouldn't have been such a big deal to Daniel. Maybe he would still be alive today. Robert never mentioned this thought to anyone, not even Janet. Although, he wondered if that same thought didn't sometimes cross her mind.

Robert laid the picture beside him on the bed and opened the book of poems. He would help Janet find a poem for Daniel's memorial. He would find the perfect poem that embodied Daniel as he looked in that picture.

Robert read poetry until he was too tired to read anymore. Finding the right poem was not going to be as easy as he thought. No wonder Janet has been spending so much time on it. He thought of Janet as he fell asleep. He missed her tonight in a way he hadn't for years. He missed the connection they used to have.

Maybe he should go back tomorrow night, instead spending the night here. After all, he did tell Janet that this trip would not be all business. Yes, he would go to the cottage tomorrow night and surprise Janet with some flowers. When was the last time he brought her flowers? Better yet, if he could get away early enough, he could stop in town and get picnic supplies. They could go on a hike, have a picnic and talk, really talk.

CHAPTER 20

Deputy Marshal Rick Sheffield sat in his office in Oklahoma City staring at the photo he just received from Carlos Sanchez. Officially the case was closed, but he never believed that Stuart Wells was dead, and he had quietly been looking for leads to his whereabouts for the past year. He found it ironic that a reporter looking for information for a story would send him Wells' picture. In this business though, you never really know where a break in the case is going to come from, especially when dealing with fugitives.

He pondered his next move. Hurricane Katrina had complicated this case. In fact, some agents at the FBI blamed him for Wells' disappearance. It's true, it was his idea to move Wells to New Orleans, but it was for his own safety.

Wells was picked up in a sweep by the Oklahoma City vice squad of gambling parlors run by the Pham family. He said he was willing to be an informant for the FBI and had evidence on a memory stick that he downloaded from the Pham's accountant's laptop that could bring tax evasion convictions on the organization's kingpins. It also contained some information that implicated several prominent citizens in bribes and kickback schemes.

But Wells didn't want to talk to the FBI initially. He insisted on getting protection from the US Marshals Service and getting the FBI to agree to several conditions before revealing the location of the evidence. The FBI wanted to see the evidence before agreeing to a deal.

Apparently, Stuart Wells had reluctantly supplied some information to the FBI before and the veracity of that information had been dubious. Wells maintained that he gave the FBI the correct location of a major ecstasy drop that was going to be attended by some of the top lieutenants of the organization. When the F.B.I. showed up for the bust, it was little more than a street deal being handled by some minor thugs.

Now, Wells was assigned to him, and he thought that it was best to get Wells out of Oklahoma City while deal negotiations continued, especially since it appeared that the sweep only netted the little fish of the operation. The Pham gang was tight; its members were very loyal. If the Pham leaders got wind that Wells was going to turn evidence, they would have him killed in jail. There were always a few gang members in there. They never turned evidence. Rick knew that it was as much out of fear as allegiance.

The Pham organization started out as a street gang committing crimes mostly against members of their own community; crimes like robbery, extortion, petty drug dealing, car theft and occasionally murder. They knew that Asian immigrants would be reluctant to go to the police. Many were in this county illegally. Others were distrustful of the government in general, and particularly the police, having seen so much corruption in their former countries. This emboldened the gang members and most crimes were committed with excessive brutality, terrorizing their victims into further silence.

Overtime, the street gang became more structured and developed a definite leadership hierarchy. They opened illegal gambling parlors, many with rigged games and prostitutes. In recent years, they started committing violent home invasion robberies against wealthy Vietnamese American families in the suburban areas. Reluctant witnesses made arrests and prosecutions hard to come by, and since the crimes affected only a limited portion of the general population, law enforcement agencies didn't allocate the resources necessary to bring down the gang.

At least that was the case until about four years ago, when the

Pham organization started branching out. The F.B.I. wasn't sure if there were some changes in the hierarchy or if the business opportunity just presented itself, but the Pham organization started trafficking ecstasy.

It is common knowledge among federal law enforcement agents that international Asian criminal groups typically smuggle powder MDMA from Europe into Canada, where it is pressed into ecstasy tablets. These groups then smuggle the tablets across the Canadian border, typically by private vehicle, supplying networks of Asian traffickers operating throughout the United States.

There had been a spike of ecstasy traffic by Vietnamese gangs throughout the United States in recent years and Oklahoma City was no exception. This resulted in an increase of violence in the general population since Caucasian males are the predominant buyers of ecstasy on the street. The F.B.I and the local police increased surveillance and arrests, but so far, they had only been able to nab lower level gang members. No one ever volunteered evidence against the Pham leadership before, until Wells.

The US Marshals Service had a contract for housing federal detainees at the Orleans Parish Prison and that seemed like a good spot to Rick to stash Wells for a week. Five days later, Hurricane Katrina battered New Orleans. When Rick realized that a major hurricane was going to hit New Orleans, he considered moving Wells to another location. But his supervisors thought that it was best to let him be evacuated with the rest of the prisoners, and then pick him up at the facility where he landed. By the time the Sheriff in charge of the Orleans Parish Prison decided not to evacuate any prisoners, it was too late to do anything about it.

The F.B.I. didn't seem too concerned about their witness. In fact, they thought that sitting out a hurricane in a prison cell might generate a little more cooperation from Mr. Wells. Of course, no one expected the levees to break; no one expected Stuart Wells to disappear without a trace.

It took three days to get all the inmates evacuated from the prison after the levees broke. It took weeks for the F.B.I. to locate all their prisoners who had been sent to other penal facilities in Louisiana.

Stuart Wells was never found.

Rick had heard stories of inmates drowning or escaping. Human Rights Watch and American Civil Liberties Union were up in arms about the inhumane treatment of the inmates during and after the storm. They claimed hundreds of prisoners were missing, having either drowned or escaped. The prison's sheriff declared that all prisoners were accounted for and that no prisoners died during the hurricane.

The official word from Washington regarding federal detainees was to stay consistent with the Sheriff's statement. There was already enough mayhem in New Orleans in the aftermath of Katrina; there was no need to alarm the public with unconfirmed reports of escaped prisoners. All federal detainees from the Orleans Parish Prison that could not be accounted for after the storm were to be listed in their files as being released prior to the date Katrina hit and presumed to have subsequently died in the hurricane or its aftermath.

Rick was never comfortable with this order, although he followed it. Even though most of the stories about inmates drowning in their cells or bodies floating through the halls came from the unit where the federal detainees were housed, Rick knew that Stuart Wells did not drown.

From the few meetings he had with Wells prior to sending him to New Orleans, he sensed that Wells had a knack for self-preservation. The research that he conducted on Wells' background after he disappeared confirmed his intuition; Wells was a survivor, and he didn't care which side of the law he had to play on to stay that way.

Rick sighed. He supposed he should fax the picture over to the FBI and see what they wanted him to do about it. That would be proper protocol. He wasn't sure if the FBI wanted Rick to find him. After all, technically, Stuart Wells was dead. But then again, Wells might still have the memory stick and Rick knew the FBI still had not been able to make a case against the hierarchy of the Pham operation. He sent the fax. He didn't really care what their answer was; he was going to bring Wells back.

Rick glanced at the clock above his door. It was getting late.

Carlos had probably left his office by now. He would call him in the morning and pump him for some more information about the story he was working on and see if he knew where the man in the picture was now. Rick would have to be careful not to sound too anxious, so Carlos wouldn't catch on that he was tracking down a fugitive. The element of surprise was going to be key in catching Wells.

He looked at the picture again and the hand written note scribbled on the bottom. Who was this "J" person? A woman, he figured; no self-respecting man would sign off a request with "XO". Most likely she is a former lover, or a close colleague of Carlos'. She seemed to be the key. He would find out who she was tomorrow as well. He knew he needed some quid pro quo to get Carlos talking. Rick looked at the first page of the fax and the information Carlos sent him on Dewayne Williams. He picked up the phone and called their Louisiana District office.

CHAPTER 21

The knock on the door startled Janet, she wasn't expecting anybody. She was in the bedroom packing a few things for her trip into her backpack. Janet stopped to fix her hair before going to answer the door, hoping that maybe it was Paul, wanting to start their little rendezvous a night early. She was halfway through the living room when she realized it was not.

Janet stopped and peered through the window panes of the door. There stood Jonathon Briggs. He raised his hand and waved at her. She made a small wave back to let him know that she recognized him. She moved slowly toward the door, allowing herself a little extra time to figure out what she should say to him.

Her first instinct was to confront him at the door as a fraud and demand an explanation. She felt betrayed. She had started to grow fond of Jonathon and considered him a friend. Now she didn't know what to believe. Was anything he told her true? Who or what was he running from?

Then she thought of Charlene and remembered that sometimes people are just running from their own mistakes and want a fresh start. After all, Janet reminded herself, she only knew who Jonathon Briggs wasn't, not who he was. And, their morning chats had seemed so genuine. Janet thought they had a real connection. He couldn't have made all of that up. She would have sensed it. No, he had been authentic with her, except for his name and background.

Janet decided to let him in and act normal. She didn't think he was dangerous. Besides, he didn't know that she had uncovered his charade. Maybe she could flush out some information about his real identity. Janet opened the door with a smile on her face.

"Good evening, Janet. Hope I'm not coming by too late. I came by earlier this afternoon, but you were out." Jonathon had in fact come by that afternoon and finding no one at home, let himself in. He searched the entire cottage and found no trace of the notebook. He took a chance that Robert would not be home this evening. He was glad that Janet was alone.

"No, it's not too late. Come on in. What did you want to see me about?"

"I needed to look at one of the books I lent you, 'The American Poet Collection'. I don't need to take it back, just want to check a poem that has been nagging at me."

"Okay, please have a seat in the living room. I think it is in the bedroom. I'll go get it."

Janet started for the bedroom and then turned back to Jonathon. "Would you like a glass of wine? I already have a bottle of red open."

"That would be lovely."

Janet went to check for the book and pour some wine. Jonathon had noted in his earlier search of the cottage that the collection book that he had lent her was not in the house. He was hoping she had taken it and the notebook together with her when she went out. Jonathon thought that it was good news that the book was in the bedroom, since most likely the notebook was there as well. He would just have to figure out a way to get into the bedroom. He smiled at the next thought that crossed his mind.

Janet returned with two glasses of wine, but no book. She handed a glass to Jonathon. "I'm sorry, Jonathon. I forgot that I let Robert take the book with him to San Francisco. I promise to bring it to you as soon as he gets back. It should only be a day, or two. In fact, I'll make a note to myself right now, so I won't forget."

Janet took a sheet of paper from the message pad and read out loud as she wrote "Return American Poem Collection to Professor Briggs ASAP," and put the note on the dining table. "There, that should do it."

"Don't worry about it. It's not like I have a deadline, just a nagging curiosity. Besides," he said as Janet sat down in the chair next to him, "it gave me an excuse to see you again. I've grown fond of our little encounters."

"Well, I guess we can have an encounter right now."

"I was hoping you'd say that." Jonathon smiled broadly, raised his glass toward Janet, and then took a sip.

Janet blushed. "Oh no, not that kind of encounter. I mean, that wasn't an invitation for that kind of encounter right now..., or later either..., right now. Not that I'm saying that that kind of encounter is unappealing. I just meant our regular encounter encounters, right now."

Jonathon chuckled softly. He liked the way she rambled on when she was flustered. It was endearing to him. Janet saw him chuckling and started laughing as well.

"I'm doing it again, aren't I? I don't know why I keep doing that with you. It sounded perfectly normal when you said it. That's what I get for trying to keep up with an English professor." Janet stopped laughing and took a sip of wine. It dawned on her that she wasn't really talking to an English professor. She liked him so much in this role that it wasn't hard for her to keep on pretending with him. But it was time to start fishing for information.

"So, Professor," Janet said sarcastically, "Tell me something about yourself. We seem to spend most of our encounter sessions talking about me."

"What do you want to know?"

"Tell me something exciting that happened in your life, something that has nothing to do with teaching English."

Jonathon thought for a moment, absentmindedly rubbing his chin with his left hand. Should he tell her his real war experience? After all, it wasn't inconsistent with anything he'd told her about Jonathon Briggs, and it might impress her. And tonight, he wanted to impress her. "Okay, I don't usually talk about it, but I was a spook in Vietnam."

"A what?"

"A spook, a spy. I was drafted into the army after graduating from college. Turns out I had a knack for learning languages besides English. I quickly became proficient in Vietnamese and Khmer, the main language in Cambodia. I spent a lot of my time recruiting local villagers to gather information about the enemy's supplies, location and movement.

Initially, I moved around a lot, traveling between South Vietnam and Cambodia, even though, technically, we weren't supposed to be in Cambodia. I either had to sneak across the border or bribe a border guard. I was pretty good at both.

Eventually, I established contact with a very reliable source in a small village in Cambodia, called Lumphat. I spent the rest of my tour there, allegedly as a missionary, teaching English and the Good Word to the villagers' children."

"That sounds fascinating, and dangerous. Were you scared?"

"I slept with a gun under my pillow every night."

"Even in Lumphat?"

"Especially in Lumphat. My source there was very reliable, and helpful to our cause, but he played both ends against the middle. He would give me up in a heartbeat, the minute I stopped being lucrative or useful to him.

In fact, sometimes the payment he required for the information he gave me was information he could give to the other side. He said he needed something so they would trust him, so he could get more for me."

"You gave out information about our own troops?"

"It was war Janet, a war that was not played by conventional rules. We never gave up much, but when we did, we always got a lot more in return. Luckily, I didn't have to make the decision on the information I gave out. That came from my field commander inside Vietnam."

"How did you communicate with him?"

"If I tell you, I will have to kill you. Or you will kill me since you said I couldn't talk about teaching English."

Janet raised one eyebrow at Jonathon. "Are you messing with me again?"

Jonathon smirked. "Well, a little, at least about the having to kill you part."

"Phew, that's a relief. Go on."

"In keeping with my cover, I sent a lesson plan each week to my 'missionary headmaster'." I listed a bible verse citation, a grammatical subject and the title of a poem that I intended to teach. Each of those items was needed to decipher the message. The numbers of the bible verse gave the key to the code I chose for that message; there was a formula to this, but I won't go into that. The grammatical subject, nouns, verbs, prepositions, etcetera signified the importance level. And the poem is where the specific information I had for them was given.

I would use a different code each time and my reader would use that code to pull out certain words or letters in the poem. The reader would have to look up the text of the poem before he could apply the code and receive my message. Instructions back to me were given in a similar fashion."

"Wow, that sounds complicated. How did you ever find poems with the right order of words or letters?"

"Well remember, I got to choose the code I used; so, for a long message sometimes I would use a simple shifting alphabet code, but basically, I read a lot of poetry!"

This was not what Janet expected to get from her fishing expedition, but at least now she understood why he knew so much about poetry for a fake professor. "I am truly amazed. I never expected a story that extraordinary. I hope you don't expect me to reciprocate because nothing in my life touches that."

"Okay I'll let you off the hook this time and go back to professorial mode. Have you discovered any new poems lately?" Jonathon purposefully made his question open-ended to see if Janet would say anything about the notebook.

"Do you mean for Daniel's bench?"

"Yes, that or just in general."

Janet found the question a little odd or at least oddly worded. He couldn't possibly know that she found Sarah's notebook, could he? No, he couldn't. She was just being paranoid. She also felt a little guilty about not spending enough time looking through the books she borrowed from him to find a poem for Daniel. She decided sarcasm was the best tactic.

Janet furrowed her brow in mock concentration. "No, nothing for Daniel yet. And, hmm let's see, new poems in general. No, at least not anything that I have a nagging curiosity about."

Jonathon laughed. "Touché, my dear."

Janet thought she would try another angle to fish for information, as long as they were being so chummy. "So, Jonathon, how did such a great catch like you end up never being married?"

Jonathon raised his eyebrow in an exaggerated look of concern. "I think the wine has gone to your head."

"Seriously, wasn't there ever a special woman in your life?"

"Actually, there was one, once. In a lot of ways, you remind me of her."

"Oh, so she was young, beautiful, intelligent, and charming,"

Janet kidded.

"Yes," Jonathon chuckled. "And she also had your modesty and sense of humor."

"Lucky girl."

"Lucky man."

"Tell me about her."

"Her name was Mai. I met her in a gambling casino. She was the waitress."

"Wait a minute, you're a gambler?"

"Was a gambler. For years after I got back from Vietnam, teaching just wasn't exciting enough. I tried fast cars and fast women, excessive drinking and extreme sports. Eventually, gambling filled the void."

"Wow, okay, go on."

"With Mai, all that changed. When she came to take my drink order I thought she seemed a little tense. I thought she looked Vietnamese, so I decided to try and lighten her mood. When she served my drink, I said to her in Vietnamese, 'What's a nice girl like you doing in a place like this?' You know, a new twist on an old line.

She looked me in the eyes with a very serious expression on her face. I thought I had offended her. She said to me, in broken English, 'Same as you, corny man, trying to make a buck,' and then she smiled and started laughing. I realized she was trying to make a joke. I laughed with her, but I couldn't take my eyes off her. Her face lit up, no, sparkled when she smiled. That smile melted my heart. I watched her all night as she worked. She didn't smile at anyone else, except me.

I came back every night for the next week. Each time, we would have longer conversations, mostly in Vietnamese since her English was not very good and I would fall more in love with her. She was engaging and witty and wise beyond her years. By the end of the week, I asked her out. From then on, whenever we weren't working, we were together.

I asked her to marry me once, but she refused. She said we didn't need marriage papers to keep us together. She told me that our hearts were already stitched together with chicken wire that would cut through our beings if we were to part.

She was right. We had two glorious years together before she died of cervical cancer. That was three years ago. I haven't dated anyone since."

"I'm sorry. You must have loved her very much."

"Yes, yes I did."

Janet noticed that the wine glasses were empty. "Would you like some more wine, Jonathon?"

"That would be nice. May I use your restroom?"

"Sure, it's in the bedroom."

As Janet headed to the kitchen to refill the wine glasses, Jonathon went into the bedroom and closed the door. He wondered if she would think he was being overly modest. He could live with that. This was most likely going to be his only chance tonight to find the notebook. It was obvious that Janet wasn't going to give anything up tonight.

He searched the room for a second time that day. He paid particular attention to any area that look like it had been disturbed since his afternoon visit. He spotted the backpack on the bed and rummaged through it. It contained only a few articles of clothing. He wondered if she were going on a trip. Perhaps she was going to join Robert in San Francisco for a day or two. Jonathon conjectured that Janet might have also given Robert the notebook to read on his trip. She did seem to have a fascination with Sarah. Maybe she wanted to show Robert some of her poetry.

In any event, the notebook was not in the bedroom or bathroom. Janet would have the notebook with her again, soon enough. He could borrow it from her then, with or without permission, at least long enough to get the code he wrote in it. Jonathon returned to the living room.

Janet was already sitting in her chair when he came back in. She handed him his glass. "This is the end of it, so if you thought you were going to come over here and get me drunk, you're out of luck." Janet joked.

"Had I known that was a possibility, I would have brought a case."

They sipped their wine and mixed small talk with flirtatious barroom banter. They were both having a good time. Neither one was in the mood any longer for covert information gathering. When the wine was gone, Jonathon noted the late hour and stood up to leave. Janet walked him to the door.

Jonathon gave Janet a sturdy hug and kissed her on the cheek before heading out the door. "I hope you don't mind; a handshake just doesn't seem appropriate anymore." He wanted to do more, but wasn't sure if she was ready, so he hesitated.

Janet gave him a hug back. Then she stepped back and took his hands in hers and smiled at him. "I'm glad you stopped by. Thanks for sharing your stories with me and I'm glad you don't have to kill me!" They both laughed and said goodnight.

Janet went to finish packing when she remembered the massage oil in the car. She went out to the car to retrieve it. The bag from the gift shop was lying on top of Sarah's notebook. She grabbed both and stuffed them in her backpack when she returned to her room. She might still want to talk with Paul about Jonathon or whoever he is. She wasn't sure. But she was sure that even though the mysterious professor may be hiding something, he was no criminal.

Jonathon strolled down the beach back toward the lighthouse. The brisk ocean breeze chilled his skin, but he felt warm inside. Red wine and Janet's company had that effect on him. He wondered if she would ever leave Robert.

CHAPTER 22

"Hello," Janet answered her cell phone and rolled over to look at the clock on the bedside table. It was 7 a.m.

"Good morning, Sunshine. Did I wake you?" Carlos asked.

"Let's just say I haven't had my morning coffee yet."

"Okay then, I know to proceed with caution."

"Ha Ha. What's up besides the fact that you forgot about the time zone difference."

"Actually, I waited an hour before calling you. I just couldn't wait any longer. You can still pick 'em kid."

"What are you talking about?"

"Your story. You're definitely on to something."

"What do you mean?" Janet sat up in bed.

"I got a call first thing this morning from my contact at the U.S. Marshal's Service. He told me he had some information on Dewayne Williams, but then, before he told me what it was, he started fishing for information about what your story was about and getting more information on that second picture you sent me.

He also wanted me to have you contact him as soon as possible, so he could assist you. A little too helpful, if you ask me. I got the distinct impression that he already knew something about the guy in that picture but wanted to see what we knew."

"Did he say he was wanted by the police?"

"No, he really didn't say anything specific, but there was something about the way he kept asking questions. Who you were? Where you were. Where you got the pictures. Where your story was set, and so on."

"What did you tell him?"

"I told him some vague stuff, just enough so he would give me the information on the Williams guy. I said you were a freelance writer working on a story about Hurricane Katrina. I said you'd been working on the story in Austin but were currently on vacation and would be back next week."

"Did you tell him my name?"

"No, I wanted to check with you first and see what you wanted me to do. He did tell me to give you his name and number if I spoke to you in California."

"How did he know I was in California?"

"I guess from the area code on the number you faxed it from."

"You didn't redact the number before you sent it to him?"

"Sorry, guess I'm getting sloppy in my old age. Besides, I didn't think the pictures were a big deal. I thought you were trying to get information for a family."

"I was, but I also told you to keep things quiet because I was looking for a new angle."

"Well, I guess you found it. Oh, and one more thing, he also knows that you are a woman whose name starts with the initial "J" and that we used to be lovers."

"What! Carlos, we were never lovers!"

"I know, but it was fun to let him think so. He thought he was so smart trying to read clues into your cryptic note on the second picture."

"You forgot to take that off too?"

"Afraid so. Anyway, I told him I'd have you call him when you got back in town. So, I guess I bought you a few days to try and find out whatever it is you are trying to uncover. But try and find it out in a hurry because, even though he said next week was fine, I get the feeling he will be hounding me until you talk to him."

"Hold on, let me get a pen." Janet reached over and opened the top drawer of the bedside table and pulled out a pen and pad of paper. "Okay, give me his name and number."

Carlos gave Janet Rick's name and phone number, and then his tone turned more serious. "Janet, do you know what you are getting into with this story?"

"Not really, but my interest is certainly piqued now." And it was, just not about the story she lied to Carlos that she was writing, but with why a U.S. Marshal was so interested in the pseudo Jonathon Briggs.

"Be careful, okay. I'm here to help if you need any 'backup'."

"Thanks, I appreciate that, but I don't think either one of us has anything to worry about."

"Well, we were lovers once you know," Carlos snickered.

"Oh, stop it," Janet laughed into the phone. "You're incorrigible." Janet was about to say goodbye when she remembered something Carlos said earlier. "Hey, Carlos, what did Rick say about Dewayne Williams?"

"Oh yeah, right. I didn't tell you that part yet. Mr. Williams was evacuated to the Hunt Correctional Center in St. Gabriel, Louisiana after Katrina. He was originally in for some domestic assault but, apparently, he got into a fight with another inmate at Hunt and ended up killing the guy; looks like he will be in prison for a long time."

"Wow, not what I expected to hear, but that's okay. Thanks, Carlos. Say 'Hello' to Betty for me and give the kids a hug from their Tia Janet."

"Will do. They would love to see you. Why don't you come over for dinner when you get back?"

"That sounds great. I'd love to."

Carlos smiled as he hung up the phone. Although he and Janet had started talking more regularly since Daniel's funeral, they both had avoided talking about his kids. He wasn't sure if it was the trip or her working again, but something has done a world of good for her

CHAPTER 23

Paul arrived to pick up Janet right on schedule. Janet grabbed her backpack and her cell phone and got in the car.

"Boy, you are a light packer." Paul said.

"You said all I needed to pack was what I needed. And I have everything I need in here."

Paul reached over and squeezed Janet's hand. "So, do I, now."

They grinned at each other like children on the initial ascent of a rollercoaster, eagerly anticipating the thrill of the ride to come. Paul started driving south on Cabrillo Highway. He explained to Janet that South Mateo County had a lot of great campgrounds.

He chose Pescadero Creek County Park because it had only a few walk-in campsites, available on a first come, first serve basis. He figured that during the middle of the week, they should have their pick, and he had the perfect remote spot in mind. They would have to hike in a half mile or so, but he promised her it would be worth it. The other great news was that it was less than an hour away, so they wouldn't be spending all their time in the car.

Janet smiled and nodded her head as Paul went on about the trails and terrain of the park, but she couldn't really focus on what he was saying. She was thinking about her conversation that morning with Carlos. Why the interest in her friendly "professor" friend and what was she going to tell Charlene? Of course, Charlene would be relieved to know that Dewayne Williams was still in prison and would be for a long time, but then what does that mean about Sarah's death?

Given the poems she found in Sarah's notebook and the autopsy showing that Sarah was pregnant, suicide was looking more and more like a possibility. Charlene had been so adamant that Sarah would not have killed herself. She dreaded showing Charlene the notebook and the report, but she knew she had to. Maybe Paul could help her with that. She would talk with him about it on this trip. But not yet, she didn't want to spoil his ebullient mood.

When they arrived at the park, they checked in at the Ranger's station. As Paul predicted, most of the campsites were still available. They parked at the trailhead, unloaded the camping gear and hiked down the trail to the campsite. Janet was awed by the coastal redwoods and Douglas fir trees as they hiked along the forest trail.

"This is really beautiful, Paul."

"I knew you would like it." Paul turned up a side path with a slight ascent. He pointed to the clearing at the top of the path. "That's our spot."

When they reached the top, they put down the gear and went about setting up camp. Janet was the first to admit that she had no camping skills, but cheerfully took on the role of assistant to Paul. Paul had set up his tent by himself a million times, but he was happy to let her hand him poles and stakes as needed.

"You'd better be careful," he told Janet. "Assisting me building things could be habit forming."

"Kind of like your massages, only not as much fun." Janet replied.

"Are you saying this isn't fun?" Paul put down his hammer in mock frustration and rushed at Janet as if he were going to tackle her. Janet let out a short shriek and ran around the tent. Paul chased after her and caught her halfway through her second lap around.

They were both laughing and breathing hard as he grabbed her around the waist, pulled her to him and kissed her. The laughing stopped and by the time they finished kissing, they were both breathless. Paul released her and went back to pick up his hammer. "Now, Ms. Assistant, let's finish putting up the tent, so I can show you how much fun setting up the inside of the tent can be."

They quickly finished putting up the tent, and then rolled out the foam pads and sleeping bags inside the tent. They unzipped the window flaps to let the breeze come through and lay down on their backs holding hands. They looked up at the tent ceiling, each pondering what the next move should be.

Janet remembered the massage oil she brought. "I have a little treat for you. I need you to take off your shirt and roll over on your stomach."

"A treat huh, well, I can go for that."

Paul followed her instructions and awaited her next move. Janet took the massage oil out of her backpack and warmed some of it up in her hands. She rubbed the oil all over his back and then deftly started to work out the kinks in his neck and shoulders.

"Oh, that's nice," Paul muttered.

"Glad you like it. It's about to get even nicer."

Janet unbuttoned her blouse and slipped off her bra. She seductively rubbed some oil on her breasts and then, lowered her torso toward him. She started at his waist, barely draping her breasts against his skin and then slowly glided them up the length of his back. By the time she reached his neck, her nipples were hard. She hugged herself against him and started rotating her torso in small circles all over his newly oiled skin.

Paul moaned softly, then kidded, "So, you're trying to one up me, are you?"

"Double upped you would be more correct," Janet retorted.

Paul rolled over on his back and pulled her down against his chest. Janet wiggled around on his chest, her breasts still slippery with the oil, her nipples hard. He placed his hands on her naked back and kissed her lustily.

Paul's cell phone rang. He ignored it. It rang again. This time he pulled it out of his pocket and checked the number. It was the church. His secretary had promised to call only if it were an emergency. "I'm really sorry, but I have to take this," he said to Janet before he answered the phone.

"Hello."

"Hi, Pastor Paul. Sorry to have to bother you on your vacation but there are two gentlemen here from the FBI who say they need to talk to you right away."

"F.B.I.? Did they say what it is about?"

"Something about a fax sent from your office yesterday. They weren't very specific. Said they would like to talk with you in person."

"I'm camping. I'll be back tomorrow evening. I will talk to them then."

"Hold on, let me tell them." Paul glanced over at Janet while he waited. They were both sitting up now. She was the only one who sent a fax yesterday. She had heard him mention the "F.B.I." She wasn't looking at him. He was about to ask her what she faxed, when his secretary came back on the line.

"Pastor Paul, they said they don't want to inconvenience you, but they do need to talk to you today. If you tell me where you are camping, they said they would come to you. They promised not to take up too much of your vacation time."

Paul sighed and brushed his hair back with his hand. "Fine, I guess. I am at the Pescadaro Creek County Park. They can stop at the Ranger station to find out which site I'm at. Tell them I'm only going to wait around for an hour, then I'm going hiking."

"Okay, I'll tell them. Sorry again, Pastor Paul."

Paul hung up the phone and turned toward Janet. "In case you haven't figured it out yet, the F.B.I. will be here in less than an hour. What in the world did you fax out yesterday?"

Janet looked up at Paul. She could hear the frustration in his tone. She wished she had said something in the car. She buttoned up her shirt as she started to explain. "I was doing some research for Charlene…"

"Charlene Monroe?"

"Yes, she asked me to check on something for her, confidentially. I was going to tell you about it later today."

"Please, tell me now."

Janet recounted what Charlene had told her about her true identity, what happened to Sarah, leaving New Orleans during Hurricane Katrina, and her suspicion that Dewayne Williams might have killed Sarah. Paul was visibly shaken. "Oh, that poor girl, she never told me. I thought I had reached her, that she trusted me, but she never told me. She must have been so scared, so ashamed. I never …." Paul put his head in his hands, took a deep breath and rubbed his face.

Janet paused for a moment and then continued her story. She told him she had no luck finding information on the internet and faxed his name and a picture she got from Charlene to a reporter friend in Austin. He had a contact in the U.S. Marshall Service who tracked down Dewayne Williams. She told Paul what Carlos had told her about Dewayne this morning. Paul thought about it for a moment and then said, "Well, I guess that is good news for Charlene, but I don't see why the F.B.I. would be interested in that."

Janet took a deep breath and blew it out. "There's more. I found something that led me to more research, and I sent a second picture to my reporter friend."

"What picture?"

"A picture of Jonathon Briggs."

"You found a picture of Jonathon Briggs? Where? Why would

you send that?"

Paul's tone was brusque. Janet pursed her lips and rubbed her hands together. She knew she had to tell him the whole story. "Actually, what I found that started me wondering about Jonathon Briggs was Sarah's notebook."

"You found Sarah's notebook?" Paul said in astonishment.

"Yes, I found it by accident."

Janet told Paul about visiting the lighthouse with Jonathon and where she found the notebook. She conveniently left out the fact that she stole the key from Jonathon's house and retrieved the book the next morning.

She explained how she kept it to read, hoping it would help her find some answers for Charlene. She always intended to give it to Charlene. In fact, she was going to ask him to go with her when she did.

Janet went on and told him about the odd poem about a professor and how that made her curious, so she did an internet search on Jonathon Briggs. She told him about finding the obituary and then turned the tables on him.

"But you already knew he was a fraud, didn't you? I found his picture in your file on him when I put Sarah's memorial file away. You told me to stay away from him, but you never explained why. From Sarah's poem I thought he might be from New Orleans. On the spur of the moment, I thought maybe Carlos's contact could get a line on him too, so I added it to my fax. I had no idea he was wanted." Janet went on to tell Paul about Carlos's conversation with the U.S. Marshall that morning.

They sat there quietly for a minute as Paul took it all in. He put his shirt back on. Finally, he asked, "Is that all?"

"No, there's one more thing you should know. Sarah's notebook contains several poems that suggest she was romantically involved with someone."

Janet paused briefly, trying to work out how to tell Paul the next part. She knew he was close to Sarah and Charlene.   She decided there was no easy way and simply said, "And I got a copy of Sarah's autopsy and it said that she was pregnant when she died."

Paul's eyes widened, then he let out a long slow whistle. "Janet, how in the world did you...," he cut himself off in mid-sentence. "Never mind, it's not important. Do you have the notebook with you?"

"Yes, I was going to show it to you while we were here."

"And the autopsy?

"It's at the back of the notebook."

"May I see them, please."

Janet reached into her backpack and pulled out the notebook. As she handed it to Paul, it dropped on the floor, flipping open to the back cover. The autopsy report spilled out. Paul picked it up and started reading it. Janet didn't want to watch him as he read.

She looked down at the floor. Her eyes fell on the open notebook. She noticed something she hadn't seen before. She leaned over to get a closer look. There on the inside of the back cover, written in blue ink in Sarah's handwriting was a heart shape with the initials P.B. inside. Below that, in a different handwriting was a citation to a bible verse and the title of a poem.

Janet picked up the book and stared at the writings. Paul finished reading the autopsy and noticed the shocked expression on Janet's face. He looked over her shoulder at the notebook.

"What is it? That doesn't look like Sarah's handwriting."

"It's not, it's a formula for a coded message and it was written by Jonathon Briggs. And I think Sarah left us a clue as to her lover."

Paul took the notebook from Janet and looked at the writing and the heart. "How do you know the bible verse and poem title are a code?"

"It's a long story, something Jonathon told me about his past."

Paul flipped back a few pages and read the poem about the professor and then flipped back some more and read some of the poems about desire and love. He shut the book, closed his eyes and pinched the bridge of his nose between his thumb and fingers. After a few minutes, he opened his eyes and grabbed her by the shoulders.

"Do you know what this means?" Paul asked her. There was an edge to his question that made Janet nervous.

"The code?"

"No, not the code, everything, everything all together – the poems, the heart, the autopsy report, the fact that Briggs wrote in her notebook." Paul didn't wait for Janet to answer before he continued. "It means that Jonathon Briggs was her lover. Think about it. She went up to the lighthouse cliff all the time. He lived right by there. In her poem she refers to him as the "*kindly* old professor" and the initials in the heart are P. B. – "Professor Briggs". The poem also shows that they had deep discussions. Oh my God, Janet, something else just occurred to me."

Paul sat down and dropped the notebook in his lap. He looked distressed. Janet knelt beside him, but she didn't touch him. She wanted to but, she couldn't. It was as if a glass wall had suddenly sprung up between them. "What? What is it?" She gently prodded.

"If Briggs wrote something on the back cover, that means he had access to her notebook, right? What if he saw the poem she wrote about him and knew she had figured something out about his identity? What if he pushed her off the cliff to keep his true identity from being discovered? What if he killed Sarah?"

Janet was stunned. That thought never occurred to her. "I don't know," she started slowly, "that's an awful lot of 'what ifs' leading to a murder charge. Even if he was her lover, that doesn't mean he killed her."

"Why are you defending him?" Paul yelled.

"I'm not defending him. I just need time to digest it all, think it through. He just doesn't seem like a murderer to me."

"Wake up Janet. The F.B.I. is on their way to see us about him right now. They wouldn't go to that kind of trouble if he wasn't a dangerous man."

Paul stood up and stormed outside the tent. Janet could hear him pacing around the campground. She couldn't help wondering about what just happened here. One minute they were on the verge of making love and then a phone call later, they were fighting. He was not just upset about Sarah; no, this was about Jonathon.

Janet recalled their hike at McNee Ranch State Park. After their encounter with Jonathon, Paul's mood soured. What was going on between those two? Certainly this couldn't all be over the bench, could it? Then it dawned on her that maybe she was the reason for renewed conflict between the two men.

A few minutes later, although it seemed like an eternity to Janet, Paul came back into the tent. He seemed calmer. He looked her in the eyes and spoke softly. "Janet, I'm sorry I snapped at you. I know that you were just trying to help Charlene and that one thing led to another. Really, I'm just mad at myself about the whole Briggs thing. I knew something was up with that man, even though he acted like a model citizen.

I should have gone to the authorities as soon as I found out he was using a dead man's identity. I warned him once, you know, that I knew he was a fake, and to stay out of the community's business. Unfortunately, that was after Sarah was already dead. No wonder he didn't want the bench up there." Paul shook his head, "Oh, I failed Sarah in so many ways."

Janet leaned her head against Paul's shoulder and sighed. Paul wrapped his arms around her and held her tightly. Janet hugged him back. She didn't speak. She was drained. This was more than she had bargained for. Straight forward adultery would have been so much easier.

"Don't worry," Paul told her, "We'll figure out what to say to Charlene and go and see her together when we get back. As for

Professor Briggs, the FBI can pick him up for now. After we meet with Charlene, we can go to the local authorities, show them what we found and let them handle the investigation.

In fact, the FBI should be here soon. Why don't I meet with them alone? No one knows that you're here with me and I know as much about the Briggs as you do. You can take your backpack and hike up the trail next to the campsite and find a pretty tree to hang out behind until they're gone. You should probably take Sarah's notebook with you too, for now."

Janet nodded in agreement. Paul slid two fingers under Janet's chin, lifted her face toward his and kissed her gently. "And when you return, we'll just lie here and hold each other until the world seems right again."

CHAPTER 24

Janet found a shady spot behind a redwood tree, a safe distance behind their campsite. She figured the shade would provide additional cover for her and allow her to peek around the tree at what was going on, without being detected. She looked back at the campsite. Paul was sitting in a folding chair, reading a book, waiting for the F.B.I. agents to arrive. They should be there soon.

She sat down and leaned against the tree. How could she have been so wrong about Jonathon; wanted by the F.B.I. and the U.S. Marshal's Service? What did he do? Was he a murderer, a terrorist, a kidnapper? None of those seemed to fit the Jonathon she knew. She knew he was liar, but was he that good of a liar? Janet thought about what Carlos had told her this morning. He thought his marshal contact knew something about the guy in the picture.

Janet rummaged through her backpack. She thought she had thrown the piece of paper with his name and number on it in the backpack this morning. She found it at the bottom of her pack. She glanced back at Paul and then dialed the number.

"Rick Sheffield," he answered.

Janet tried to sound casual, which was difficult since she was talking in a hushed tone. "Hello, Marshal Sheffield. This is Janet Reed. I'm a friend of Carlos Sanchez. You told him to give me your number, said you might be able to help me with a story I'm working on."

"Yes, Janet, I'm sorry, what did you say your last name was?"

"Reed"

Rick wrote down her name. "Reed, okay. Thanks. I thought you were on vacation, didn't expect to hear from you so soon."

"Well I had a few minutes, so I thought I would call."

"Can you speak up? I'm having trouble hearing you."

"Sorry," Janet lied, "I'm in the library."

"That doesn't sound like a fun vacation. So, tell me about your story. I was able to find out some information on Mr. Williams for you, but I need more background information on the fellow in the second picture to be able to help you there."

Janet saw two men dressed in black walking up the trail toward the campsite. She had hoped to coax some information about Jonathon out of Marshal Rick Sheffield, but she was running out of time. She would have to get straight to the point.

"Listen, I would love to play the game with you, where you try and get information out of me and I try and get information out of you, and we're both clever and flirty on the phone, but quite frankly, I don't have time right now. How about we just make a deal? If you tell me what you know about that guy, I will tell you what I know."

"Hey, I was just trying to help you out with your story. I don't know anything about this guy."

"Oh, really, then why are two F.B.I. agents coming to talk to my friend right now about a fax I sent from his office, a fax about the guy in the picture?"

"What? The F.B.I.? Are you sure?" Rick was puzzled. Jim Fletcher, Assistant Special Agent in Charge of the F.B.I. field office in Oklahoma City had called him personally this morning and said Rick should follow up on this lead, find Wells and bring him in. He told Rick to "keep it under the radar" until he had Wells in custody and the F.B.I. decided how they were going to proceed.

Rick told Fletcher that his source was on vacation in California and might not contact him for a week but thought that Wells was probably in Texas somewhere. Fletcher told him that one more week didn't really matter after all this time.

Rick's mind started racing, his face got hot. Those bastards, he thought. They are trying to track Wells down themselves and make the collar. It is my case and my lead; those two faced, glory seeking, poachers. Rick was not going to let them beat him on this one. The F.B.I. was trying to track down Janet to locate Wells. He had Janet on the phone right now. If Wells was in Texas, he could go down there and pick him up today, while they were still talking to her in California.

"Okay, Janet, I'll make a deal with you. I'll tell you why I am interested in this fellow, if you tell me where he is before you tell the F.B.I."

"Why, is he that big of a prize that y'all are fighting over who gets to bring him in? What did he do?"

"It's not so much what he did, as what he knows." Rick went on to tell Janet about Stuart Wells' arrest in the gambling sting and his subsequent offer to turn over information which implicated some of the hierarchy of the Pham crime organization. He also told her how he was assigned to Wells' case and how they lost track of him after Hurricane Katrina. "Officially, he is listed as dead in our files. But I knew he was still out there."

"So, are you trying to find Stuart Wells so that he can be a witness or to put him back in jail for his crimes?" Janet repeated Jonathon's real name in her head. Stuart Wells, it did fit him, but she still liked Jonathon Briggs better. Whatever his name was, she didn't want to see him go to jail.

"Well I guess that depends on him. I could put him in our witness protection program if he wants to cooperate. But it's my job to bring him in and keep him in protective custody until we figure that out. Now, Janet, tell me what you know."

"Okay, fair enough. He's living under the name of Jonathon Briggs near an old lighthouse, in a small resort area, south of San Francisco on the San Mateo peninsula."

"He's in California?" Rick grabbed his car keys, checked that his pistol was in his shoulder holster and headed out the door as he continued talking to Janet on his cell phone.

"Listen Janet, I'm going to the airport right now to catch a flight out there. I want you to wait for me and then take me to him."

"You want me to set him up?" Janet did not like the turn this conversation was taking.

"No, it's not like that. I'm interested in his safety. We're not the only ones interested in finding him, you know. If the Pham organization gets wind that he's not dead, they'll find him and kill him."

"Oh, I hadn't thought about that. And of course, you still want to beat the F.B.I. agents, who are already here."

"Okay, fine. So, what is the closest airport to you?"

"The closest major airport is in San Francisco, but I think there is also a small airport in Half Moon Bay."

"Okay, I'll meet you at the library in Half Moon Bay, as soon as I can."

Janet peeked around the tree at the campsite. The two agents were talking with Paul. One of them was showing Paul a copy of the fax with Jonathon's picture and her note. "I don't think you need to rush. The F.B.I. agents are talking to my friend right now."

"Yeah well, if your friend tells the F.B.I. who you are, and they come visit you, just stall them for a while or say you don't know where Wells lives."

"He won't tell them who I am, but he will tell them where Jonathon, I mean Wells, lives."

"He knows him too?"

"Yeah, and he would be happy for him to be locked up."

"Why?"

"It's a long story."

"Well, I'm still coming. I'll sort it out with the F.B.I. when I get there."

Another thought occurred to Rick. Maybe Janet could identify the agents for him, and then he could call them and tell them to hold off on picking up Wells until he got there. He knew most of the Oklahoma agents.

"Janet, did you happen to get a look at the F.B.I. agents?"

"I'm looking at them right now."

"Can you describe them to me?"

"One is dressed in a dark suit, with a shirt but no tie. He's wearing dark sunglasses and has dark hair, slicked back against his head. He's probably five foot eleven. The other agent has on dark pants, a tight black T-shirt, and a chain necklace. It looks like he works out and wants people to notice it. He also has on dark sunglasses, so I can't see much of his face. He has short black hair that is spiked up with gel. He's several inches shorter than the other guy."

"They don't sound like Oklahoma boys. They must be California agents, although I don't see why they would involve the California folks on something that was no rush and supposed to be done 'under the radar'."

"Excuse me?"

"Sorry, just thinking out loud." Rick still didn't see why the F.B.I. jumped on this so quickly, especially when they knew it was his case. It's not like he was some rookie or incompetent. Rick had a solid career record at the U.S. Marshal's Service and a good reputation with other federal agencies. No, something else was up.

What was it about Wells? Rick never got very much information out of him. He had been cagey in those first few interviews. The only thing Wells had been adamant about was that he was not going to talk to the F.B.I. until a deal had been cut and he would be guaranteed protection by the Marshal Service. He knew there was bad blood between the F.B.I. and their informant but this was outside of protocol, didn't make sense…unless…of course, that's why they could never make a case against the big fish. Rick stopped walking.

"Janet, can you tell me what race the agents are?"

"Hard to tell on the taller guy, medium complexion, medium build. Could be some sort of mixed races, part Asian, part I'm not sure. But the other guy is definitely Asian."

"Damn! Why didn't I think of this before! Janet, listen to me very carefully. I don't want you to panic, but there is a good chance that those men are not F.B.I. agents. I think they are hit men, sent by the Pham organization to kill Wells."

"What? How would they know about him?"

"I'm starting to think that someone in the local F.B.I. office leaked it to them. I think that Wells knows that there's a leak and that's why he wanted to go through my office first."

"But…"

Rick cut her off and continued, "We don't have time to analyze that now. You must make sure they don't know who you are and that you know who they are. They are dangerous men and will kill anyone who gets in their way. If you and your friend are in a public library, you're probably both safe, especially if your friend still believes they are agents and he is cooperating."

"Actually, I lied to you earlier. We're not at the library. We're at an isolated campsite at Pescadaro Creek County Park. They came out here to talk to my friend because I faxed it from his office. I'm hiding in the woods."

"Okay, stay hidden. Wait for them to leave. Do you have a number for Wells, so I can warn him?"

Janet cell phone started beeping. She pressed the cell phone tightly against her chest and sank back behind the tree. God, what if they heard that. She whispered into the phone to Rick, "My battery's going out. I don't think he has a phone. He lives behind a light house, a little north of Half Moon Bay. Marshal? Rick?"

There was no answer, the battery was dead. She didn't know what, if any part, of her directions he heard. Shit! What was she going to do now? She knew Paul was down there giving directions to Jonathon's house to men who were going to kill him. This was all her fault. Why did she send that picture?

Maybe Paul hadn't told them yet. Maybe she could find a way to trick them or beat them to Jonathon's house and warn him. She couldn't just sit here hiding and let him die. Janet picked up her backpack and walked down the hill to the campsite.

CHAPTER 25

All three men looked up at her as she approached. They all looked startled. Paul's expression changed to perplexed as Janet started to talk in her best Southern Belle drawl.

"Well, I guess I'm not the hearty outdoorsman I thought I was. Oh, hi there." Janet nodded at the other men and looked at Paul. "Sorry Paul, I forgot you were expecting visitors."

She looked back at the agents. "Excuse me gentlemen, I need to get the car keys from Paul. It seems I cannot heed the call of nature out in nature, if you know what I mean. Maybe you don't; guys seem to have no problem with that. Guess it's a girl thing. Anyway, I'm going to have to drive back down to the civilized campground and use their facilities. Normally I wouldn't be this rude and interrupt but it's kind of an emergency."

The startled look on the two men's faces now changed to smirks as they glanced over at each other. Paul reached into his pants pockets and handed Janet the keys. Janet took the keys and started down the path toward the car.

She had hoped that Paul would figure out something was up and excuse himself to talk with her for a second or offer to go with her. All he did was just hand her the keys. He didn't even comment. He was probably embarrassed, thought that she really is a camping wimp and has to use the facilities. It occurred to Janet that Paul really didn't know her very well. Carlos, hell, even Robert, would have picked up on the signals she was sending.

Now what was she supposed to do? Take the car and go warn Jonathon and leave Paul there? What if the other men got suspicious when she didn't return? What if they intended to kill Paul after he gave them the information they wanted, because he could identify them? It would be easy out here in the wilderness, with no witnesses. Janet turned around and walked back to the campground. Again, she put on the Southern Belle routine. Men tended to underestimate her that way.

"Excuse me again. So sorry, but, Paul, I realized that your car is a standard and I can't drive a stick shift. Could you gentlemen please let me borrow him for just a few minutes, so I could, you know, take care of business? I promise to bring him right back."

"We're almost done here, can't you wait a few more minutes?" Paul said to Janet in an exasperated tone.

Janet looked him in the eye trying to convey a silent message with a pleading look. "I really can't. I'm getting desperate and I only packed this one pair of jeans."

The two men were choking back laughter. The taller one suggested that they all walk out together and finish their talk with Paul while Janet used the "facilities."

"Great idea," Janet said, and she rushed over and grabbed Paul's hand and pulled him down the path, before he had a chance to reply. She wanted to keep up her appearance as a desperate woman as the two other men followed behind them. It wasn't hard to do. In fact, the hard part was controlling how desperate she really was.

Paul was silent until they got in the car and started driving toward the main campground. "What's the matter with you?"

"Paul listen to me; those men are not F.B.I. agents. They're hit men sent to kill Jonathon."

"Please, be serious Janet. Why in the world..."

"I called the number for the U.S. Marshal that Carlos gave me this morning while I was in the woods. Jonathon was going to give evidence about an Asian crime family before he disappeared. The Marshal thinks someone in the F.B.I. leaked that Jonathon is alive to them and they came here to find whoever sent the fax so they could find out where he is and kill him. Did you tell them where he lives yet?"

"I told him he lived by the old lighthouse north of Half Moon Bay. I was about to give them specific directions when you came out of the woods." Paul pulled up to the campground restrooms.

"Okay, I've got to go inside the restroom, so they don't think I'm on to them. Quick, give me your cell phone."

"It's back at the campground."

"Damn. Okay, I'll think of something. You go talk to them but give them the wrong directions to Jonathon's house and don't let them know that you know they are not agents or they might kill us too."

"Janet, I don't know if ..."

"Please, Paul, just do it."

Janet got out of the car and rushed into the ladies' room. She climbed up on the sink and peered out of the small window near the top of the wall at the two cars parked outside. Paul and the other men got out of the cars and walked over to a picnic table on the side of the building. Janet climbed down and went to the door. She had to find a way to give her and Paul some lead time to get to Jonathon's. If she could sneak out and somehow sabotage the men's car, that could do it.

Janet peaked around the corner. The table the men were seated at was to the left of the entrance. The two men sat opposite Paul, facing toward her. The man in the suit was writing down directions, the other man was looking around. A pickup truck with a noisy muffler drove down the camp road. The men looked up at it. This was her chance.

Janet exited the restroom, hugging her body against the outside wall and quickly slipped behind the building. She stopped and glanced around the corner of the building at the men. They had gone back to talking. They had not seen her.

Janet hurried around the building to the other side. There were just a few feet of open space between the side of the building and the far side of the men's car. Janet had to get over there without being seen. She thought about just casually strolling over, but the short guy was still looking around and would wonder what she was doing hanging out around their car. She had to try something else. Paul would be finished soon, so she was running out of time.

Janet took a deep breath and crouched down so that she was below the level of the hood and scurried across the open space. She didn't know if she had been spotted but couldn't worry about that now. She undid the cap on the tire valve stem and pressed her fingernail down into it. Air started leaking out slowly. She jammed her fingernail down harder. The air escaped faster.

Janet's heart was racing. They could come back to the car any moment. What would she say if she got caught? There would be no talking her way out of this one. They would be on to her. She and Paul, and Jonathon would be dead. God, this was stupid idea. What was she thinking? Why didn't she stay hidden until they left, like she was told?

Janet heard the voices of the men growing louder. They were talking about the weather. They must have finished getting the directions and were heading back to the cars. Janet looked under the car to see where their feet were. They were heading toward the front of the cars. She quickly replaced the cap and scampered around to the back of the car, keeping low and close to the vehicle. The three men stopped in front of Paul's car. Janet froze.

"Well, I guess your lady friend really did have a need for these facilities," Janet heard one of the men joke.

"Yeah, I don't know what is taking her so long. It would be just my luck to bring her on a romantic camping trip and she develops 'woman problems' or something." Paul said sarcastically.

The other men laughed. Janet did not think it was humorous but hoped that Paul would keep them engaged while she sneaked over to get behind Paul's car.

"Actually, as long as we're here, I think I'll duck in for a second before we hit the road," one of the men said.

"Good idea, think I will too," the other one added. "Thank you, Pastor, for your assistance. Enjoy the rest of your vacation."

Janet watched the two men's feet from underneath the car. When she saw them enter the men's room, she popped up and ran over to Paul. She motioned to him to be quiet and they got in the car.

"Quick, let's get going," Janet said urgently to Paul.

"Okay, Okay." Paul started backing out and turned to go down the road back to the campsite.

"No, No," Janet yelled, "We have to leave the park and head back to town right now."

"Janet, calm down. I just want to get my things before we go. I gave them wrong directions, so we have plenty of time to stop by the campsite before heading back."

"If we go back there, they will kill us."

"Why, I did like you said and played along with their act. They have no reason to suspect that we know anything."

"As soon as they come out of that restroom they will."

"What? Why?"

"I let the air out of one of their tires."

CHAPTER 26

Paul was fuming as they sped down the highway. He hadn't said a word to Janet since they left the campground. She had started with more explanations, but he asked her to be quiet. He wanted to collect his thoughts, figure out a logical way to handle all of this before they reached town.

Janet couldn't sit still. She kept alternating between looking behind them for signs of the hit men's car and rummaging through her backpack, looking for one thing or another. First, she searched for her phone charger. She had thrown one in, but it was the one from the house, not the car charger. Next, she looked for Rick Sheffield's number. When she located the paper this time, she stuffed it in her pocket. Finally, she took out Sarah's notebook and started frantically flipping through it. Paul couldn't stand it any longer.

"What are you doing?"

"I'm looking to see if Jonathon wrote anything else in Sarah's book; something that might provide the marshal with a clue to the F.B.I. leak or something else about the crime organization."

"I don't see what good that is going to do now. First of all, I doubt that there is anything like that in there; second, you can't contact him, even if you did find something; and third, we will probably be dead before you have a chance to turn the notebook over to anyone anyway."

Paul immediately regretted saying those last words. Janet closed the book and put in back in her backpack. Her eyes brimmed with tears.

"Paul, I'm so sorry. I didn't know any of this would happen. I just wanted to know the truth about him. You were so upset by him, but he was so nice to me. I'm sorry I put you in danger back there. I just didn't want to be responsible for someone's death. I…"

Paul reached over and squeezed her hand. "It's okay. Don't worry; we're not going to die. I was just venting. What you did probably saved my life. You could have left me there at the campsite and taken off. Who knows, they might have decided to kill me out there in the wilderness all by myself."

Janet nodded. Paul continued, "I have been thinking about how to get us out of this and I think we should go straight to the police and tell them what we know and let them go pick up Briggs, or whoever he is. He'll be safe in jail until your marshal friend gets here."

"That sounds good, but I don't think it'll work. By the time we go into the station, explain everything to them and they send a patrol car over, those other men will have had time to figure out where Jonathon is and kill him. No, we must go and get Jonathon and then bring him to the police station. We should have time for that."

"What if he won't come with us?"

"He will if he knows he's being hunted by the Pham family, don't you think?"

"He could run and hide somewhere else. It not like he hasn't done that before. And with this new evidence we just found about Sarah's death, I'm not sure we should take that chance."

"I'd rather take that chance than know I could have prevented a death and didn't try. Besides, after we warn him, if he doesn't come with us, we can still go straight to the police and tell them everything we know about him."

"But why should we risk our lives to save his. He's a criminal. I still think it's too dangerous. Let him fend for himself until the police get there."

"Paul, we have to warn him, otherwise we are signing his death warrant. Even if he is guilty, he at least deserves his day in court."

"Janet, why do you always defend him?!"

"I'm not defending him! I'm just not willing to be judge, jury and executioner. You're a pastor; you're supposed to be compassionate. Why do you hate him so much?"

"I don't hate him. I just haven't bought into his con like you and the rest of the town has. And I care more about your safety than his. He could be as big a threat to you as those other men. What if he takes you as a hostage?"

"He won't harm me. I know that for sure."

"No, you don't. Everything he has ever told you has been a lie."

"You're wrong. And if you won't go with me, then I will go warn him myself. Just drop me off at the cottage."

Janet turned and looked out the window. She didn't want to discuss it anymore. They were almost to the cottage anyway. Paul looked straight ahead and drove faster. Janet turned around to check and see if they were being followed and noticed that Paul drove right past the road to her cottage.

"Hey, what are you doing?"

"I know a shorter way to reach Briggs' place, through the woods off a cul-de-sac up the road a bit. We can get to him faster that way."

Janet turned and faced Paul, "We?"

"Well you didn't really think I was going to let you go alone did you?"

Janet reached over and laid her hand on his forearm, "Thank you, Paul."

Paul turned left off the main road into a cul-de-sac and parked.

"Okay, we're here. Follow me. It's about a half a mile in."

Janet and Paul jumped out of the car and raced through the woods, with Paul leading the way. Paul stopped about 50 yards from the house to let Janet catch up with him. She stopped, bent over and put her hands on her knees, trying to catch her breath.

"Let me do the talking," she said between pants as they started walking toward the back of the house.

Jonathon opened the back door before they reached the porch.

"Jonathon, you have to come with us right now," Janet insisted as soon as she saw him. "We don't have much time. I'll explain in the car."

"And where are we going?" Jonathon inquired, not moving from his doorway.

"There are some men, not far behind us that want to kill you. If we leave now, we can go to the police before they come," Janet continued.

"What men, what did they look like?"

"Look Briggs, or Wells or whoever you are," Paul broke in. "We know who you are and there are two Asian hit men who know who we are and that you live in this area. We came to warn you, now let's get the hell out of here. We can discuss it at the station."

"Where did you park?" Jonathon asked Paul.

"Look, I don't see what difference that…"

"Where did you park and do they know what your car looks like?" Jonathon yelled over Paul as he spoke.

"Yes," Janet answered. "They know what Paul's car looks like and we parked it in a cul-de-sac off the main road."

"Quickly, get in the house," Jonathon ordered. "We'll leave the front way and go down to Janet's car. It'll be safer. It's too easy to spot a car from that cul-de-sac."

Janet walked into the house. Paul hesitated. "Suit yourself," Jonathon said as he turned and went inside. Paul reluctantly decided that Jonathon had a good point and followed him inside and closed the door.

Jonathon was already quizzing Janet as Paul entered the living room. "What did they look like?" Janet gave a brief description of the men to Jonathon. "How far behind you are they?"

"How ever long it took them to change a tire?" Janet answered. Jonathon raised one eyebrow at her answer.

"I let the air out of one of their tires." Janet explained.

Jonathon chuckled, "Isn't she great?" he said to Paul. Paul just glared at him, stone-faced.

"Okay," Jonathon said, continuing his assessment. "That means they're not far behind, and you're right, they're dangerous. You two go out the front and head as quickly as you can to Janet's car. I've got to grab something, then I'll be right behind you. Janet, take the tool that opens the lighthouse with you. If you see trouble, you can hide out there. I know you know how to use it."

Jonathon headed off toward his bedroom. Janet went to the bookshelf, snatched the tool from the box, stuffed it in her pocket and hurried out the door. Paul stood there momentarily motionless, trying to determine which one to follow. Janet called to him as she headed down the path. He ran out after her.

As Janet rushed down the path toward the lighthouse, the trees seemed to blur together. It reminded her of watching the fence posts run together when she was young, and her father would speed down the ranch road to her grandparent's house. She turned around to look at Paul as he caught up with her. When she turned back, she was yanked off her feet.

The short Asian man with the spiked hair had grabbed her from behind a tree and was now holding her off the ground in a bear hug. She struggled against his hold but couldn't move an inch. Janet watched helplessly as Paul was attacked by his partner.

Although Paul was bigger than his assailant, he was no match for the lightening quick blows the other man was landing on Paul's body with his fists and feet. After a few minutes, Paul was on ground, curled up in the fetal position, his fisted hands and forearms pressed against his own head in an effort to ward off any remaining blows. Paul's attacker stopped striking him and stood looking down over him for a second. Then he straightened out his suit coat, smoothed his hair back along his head with both hands and turned to face Janet.

Janet, who was still dangling off the ground in her captor's grip, was at his eye level. He looked at her with a fixed stare and asked calmly, "Where is he?"

"I don't know," Janet stammered. "We were just in his house and he wasn't there."

The man in the suit kept his eyes locked on hers. "You lie too much," he said as he reached over and nailed a swift upper cut between her legs. Janet groaned and doubled over in pain.

The spiked haired man released her, and she dropped to the ground. "I bet you really have to pee your pants now," he laughed.

Paul pushed himself up to a seated position. "Leave her alone."

The man in the suit turned back to Paul, took a gun out of his coat and pointed it at Paul's head. "Where is Wells?"

"He's in the house, or at least he was. He's probably long gone by now. The bastard used us as bait."

"Chien, go check the house," he commanded. He motioned with his gun for Paul to move over next to Janet. "If either of you moves or makes a sound, I'll shoot you both."

Chien pulled out his gun and circled the outside of the house before he entered through the back door. Janet and Paul clung to each other and, along with the man in the suit, silently stared at the lifeless house.

They were still watching for any sign of activity inside the house when they heard a gun cock. They turned to see Jonathon standing behind the man in the suit with a gun pushed up against his back. "Hello, John, nice of you to stop by for a visit after all this time. I know how busy you are."

John Nguyen was a top lieutenant in the Pham organization despite his relatively young age. He was smart and ruthless and quickly gained the confidence of the head of the organization, "Uncle Bao." It was John Nguyen's connections with a cousin in Vancouver that got them into the lucrative ecstasy trafficking trade.

Jonathon had run across John Nguyen several times over the years. He was cold and calculated and skilled at getting people to talk. He was overly ambitious and at times, unnecessarily brutal. Jonathon recalled one incident in particular.

It was several months after Mai died. He overheard some of the gamblers speaking in Khmer about an attack on a Cambodian family in their home in Bethany. Apparently, the father kept money from his restaurant at the house. Some masked men had broken in and tortured the family until he turned over the money.

Jonathon was horrified as he listened to the details of the attack. One of the daughters was raped even after all the money was turned over. Jonathon became physically ill when he heard them mention the name Phirun Neak. Three days earlier he had given that name to John Nguyen.

Jonathon hadn't been reported any information on his clients in the months after Mai died and Uncle Bao sent John Nguyen over to remind him that providing information on what he heard was part of his agreement with Uncle Bao. Mai's death didn't change that.

So, Jonathon passed along that he overheard a Cambodian man talking about how his boss took cash home from the restaurant in take-out boxes every night. He thought that they would just rob him outside the restaurant and then start taking protection money. That's what they used to do.

After hearing what John Nguyen did at the Neak's house, Jonathon realized that Uncle Bao's new lieutenant was out of control and he had to find a way out.

About six months later, his break came. After the Pham organization's accountant stopped by to transfer Jonathon's figures for the week to his laptop, he decided to stay and gamble. Jonathon offered to lockup the laptop in his office for safe keeping and made sure the girls brought the accountant some stiff drinks and paid him a lot of attention.

Ten minutes was all it took for Jonathon to break his password and download the incriminating information. He waited a few more months to make sure his download was not detected and then anonymously leaked information to the local police to set up the raid on his gambling lounge.

"Hello Stuart, Uncle Bao sends his regards," John Nguyen said casually, in spite of the fact that the barrel of a gun was pressed into his back.

"Drop your gun, slowly," Jonathon quietly demanded. John Nguyen complied. Jonathon kicked it to the side of the path out of John Nguyen's reach, as he continued talking. "Janet. Paul. I want you to get up and make your way down the path. Stay behind the trees, out of any line of fire from the house."

"No need to worry about your friends. We just want to talk with you. Uncle Bao has been worried about you." John Nguyen started.

"Actually, I have a deal for Uncle Bao. And I'll be happy to discuss it with you after my friends have left."

Janet and Paul stood up, gingerly slipped behind the trees and started walking backwards away from the house and the two men. As they passed close to where the gun lay at the side of the path, Paul decided to go over and retrieve it for additional protection.

Paul stepped out into the path and reached down to pick up the gun. Suddenly, from out of the woods, a ka bar knife sailed through the air and pierced Paul's hand, pinning it to the ground in front of the gun. Paul dropped to his knees and screamed in agony. Janet shrieked and jumped behind a tree.

Jonathon pulled John Nguyen closer to shield himself and moved the gun up and pressed it hard against John's temple. "Tell him to come out of the woods, with his arms up or you're a dead man."

John Nguyen shouted the command in Vietnamese to Chien. There was no response. He started talking again in English. "Stuart, you should know that Chien is an excellent marksman. His gun is most likely trained on your friend's head at this moment. He could shoot him dead before you could pull the trigger on me. His next shot would be at you, through me if necessary. And the girl, well, he would shoot her too, eventually."

Jonathon scanned the horizon. He did not see Chien anywhere. "True, the Pastor will be dead before I can react, but that doesn't bother me much. But I think you underestimate your value to the family. They do not want you dead. Tell Chien to come out and we'll make a deal. No one needs to die today."

John Nguyen again shouted to Chien to come out of the woods. This time Chien shouted that he was coming out. He was closer than Jonathon expected. When Chien stepped out the woods onto the path, Jonathon's heart dropped. Chien held Janet up against his body with one arm. His other hand held a gun to her head.

"Yes, Stuart, you're right. No one needs to die today," John Nguyen said unemotionally. "Let's make a deal, it's up to you."

Paul stretched his left arm across his body, trying to reach the gun that lay on the other side of his pinned hand. Chien cocked his gun. Paul stopped moving, he looked up at Jonathon. Jonathon had been willing to play games with Paul's life. He couldn't do the same with Janet's.

"Okay," Jonathon said looking at Chien. "We are going to both lower our weapons slowly on the count of three. Then you release the girl and I will release John. After that, we can talk. I have not dishonored the family."

Jonathon slowly started counting to three. He locked eyes with Chien. As he started to pull the gun away from John Nguyen's head, Chien followed suit with Janet. By the third count, both men's guns were pointed toward the ground.

In a split-second John Nguyen jumped into action. He slammed his head backwards into Jonathon's face and then spun around and crashed his bent elbow into his temple. Jonathon fell to the ground unconscious.

John Nguyen picked up Jonathon's gun and tucked it in his pants. Then he went over to retrieve his own gun still lying next to Paul's knifed hand. He pulled the knife out of Paul's hand, yanked him to his feet and pushed his gun into Paul's ribs.

"Let's bring them in the house and tie them up," John Nguyen said to Chien in Vietnamese. "We need to get what we came for before we kill them."

CHAPTER 27

The smell of the fresh meat and herbs in the delicatessen invigorated Robert. Jack had no problem with Robert leaving early today. In fact, he recommended that Robert stop at this delicatessen on the way to the cottage. "They have the freshest meats and produce and a great selection of chilled wines," Jack told Robert before he left his office.

Robert ordered a few sandwiches and got a fruit and chocolate platter for dessert. He picked out a brightly colored bouquet of flowers and two chilled bottles of expensive California chardonnay and went to the checkout counter. He took a deep breath in. God, it smelled good in here. He felt great. There was certain thrill in planning this surprise for Janet. The anticipation he felt about their afternoon of bonding, both mentally and physically, just added to his excitement. He vowed to himself to do this sort of thing more often.

When he drove up to the cottage, he was happy to see that Janet's car was there. He picked up the bags of food and wine with one hand, held the bouquet in the other, and rushed to the cottage door. "Brace yourself, my dear Janet," Robert said under his breath. "You are about to be swept off your feet for the second time in your life."

Robert thought about the first time. He and Janet had been dating for just over a month, although between his work schedule and the demands on her as a young reporter, they didn't get to spend a lot of time together. Still, the time they did spend together was fabulous and Robert thought she might be the one. He wanted to kick it up to the next level, seal the deal, so to speak.

So, he planned a surprise, romantic get-away. He enlisted Carlos to arrange for Janet to have the weekend off but to tell her that she was going on a special overnight assignment in the hill country and to pack an overnight bag. Carlos told Janet that a driver was picking her up at noon on Friday.

Janet was surprised when the driver turned out to be Robert but figured out what was going on when Carlos winked at her as she got in the car. That weekend turned into a cherished memory for both Robert and Janet.

Robert had planned every detail, scripting the entire weekend for maximum romance. He booked them at a bed and breakfast in Fredericksburg that was really a series of old log cabins that had been refurbished inside. He arranged for them to have the most secluded cabin by the meadow and to have breakfast left in a basket on the door each morning.

On the way to the cabin, he pulled into a nearby winery and they spent the afternoon sitting on the tasting room patio, drinking wine and gazing at the vineyard and surrounding lavender fields, which were in bloom. Although, to be honest, Robert spent more time gazing at Janet, than at anything else.

They went into town right after checking in, since Robert had reservations for dinner. Robert was glad when Janet said she loved the charm of the old cabin. He figured that this would impress her more than a suite at the Four Seasons.

Robert suggested that they duck into the bar next to the restaurant for a quick drink before dinner. Janet ordered more wine and Robert ordered a scotch and then excused himself for a moment. No sooner had Robert left, then a tall man appeared, dressed in jeans with a tuxedo coat and wearing a top hat. He presented a dozen red roses to Janet. "Madam," he addressed her, "Mr. Reed would like you to join him out back. I will escort you."

Janet followed the man in the top hat through the bar and out of the back door, wondering what the heck Robert was up to. To her delight, she saw Robert standing next to a horse drawn carriage. He helped her into the carriage, roses in tow, and the driver drove them through town.

Fredericksburg, Texas is a quaint little town, settled by German immigrants in the mid-1800s. With its cobblestone streets, beautiful old churches, German pubs and shops along Main Street, it still has a certain old-world charm. Janet marveled at all the sights as they were squired through town in their carriage. But this time, if truth be told, Janet mostly had eyes for Robert.

When they arrived back at the cabin after dinner, both of their heads were swimming; intoxicated more on the giddiness of new found love than the wine they had with dinner. Robert kissed her as he lifted her up and carried her to the bed. Robert was pleased with himself. Everything had turned out exactly as planned. That's when Janet changed the script.

"Have you ever danced naked in the moonlight," Janet asked him, as she slowly unbuttoned his shirt. "I noticed that there's a full moon tonight."

At first Robert was hesitant. Except for skinny dipping at summer camp, he had never been naked outdoors, and certainly not in public. Besides, they didn't have a radio and there was a nice soft bed inside waiting for them.

But Janet was persuasive. She seductively stripped off her clothes and the rest of his and led him outside. "What's the use of having a secluded cabin, if you don't take advantage of it," she cajoled him as he stalled on the porch. "Come on, no one can see us, except the wood nymphs and the love gods. And look, they put a spotlight out for us," Janet teased some more as she escorted him to a spot by the meadow where a moon beam was shining.

At first, Robert stood there amused and fascinated, as he watched Janet prance around in the moonlight singing the chorus from the James Brown classic "I Feel Good". She was a free spirit, and a beautiful one at that. The moonlight seemed to accentuate her athletic shape; reflecting off her full, round breasts, highlighting the soft curves of her firm bottom, and flashing on the lightly rippled muscles of her abdomen as she moved.

As Robert continued to watch her dance, he was drawn to more than just her body; the unpretentious way she was caught up in her own dance, the rhythmic movement of her arms and fingers, the sparkle in her eyes when she smiled at him.

Soon he was dancing too. They sang songs out loud to each other while they danced; sometimes solo, sometimes together. They didn't always get the lyrics right, but they didn't care. Gradually, the singing turned into humming, and the dancing into kissing and touching. Then leisurely, tenderly, they made love in the soft grass by the meadow, and Robert knew he had found the woman he wanted to spend the rest of his life with.

They spent the rest of the weekend in the cabin, making love, talking, drinking the wine they bought at the winery, eating only the fruit, and muffins left on their door each morning. But each night, in the wee hours, they came outside and danced together, naked in the moonlight.

Robert smiled and shook his head back and forth as he came out of his reverie. He knocked on the door and placed the hand with bouquet behind his back. He waited for a minute and then went in. "Janet," he called out. "Janet, I came home early. I have a surprise for you."

The house was quiet. She must be out for a walk, he thought. He went to the kitchen and put the groceries down. He found a vase for the bouquet, filled it with water and arranged the flowers. He looked around for a good place to put them so she would see them when she came in the door.

He decided the dining room table would be the best spot. When he put them down, he noticed the note on the table. It was Janet's handwriting. She was always leaving notes for herself or him. He picked it up and read it. "Return American Poem Collection to Professor Briggs ASAP."

Robert thought that the title sounded familiar; it might be the title of the book Janet gave him to read. He went out to the car to look in his briefcase. Sure enough, that was the book. He wondered if Janet left the note for him. Where did Janet say he lived? He believed she said he lived somewhere behind the lighthouse. That's probably where Janet was, sitting on the bench by the lighthouse. Robert knew she liked it up there. Robert decided to hike up to the lighthouse with the book.

He went back to the kitchen and put the food and one bottle of wine in the refrigerator. He opened the other bottle and poured a glass. He put the glass on the table next to the flowers and wrote a note to Janet on the back side of her note, in case she wasn't up there and returned before he did. "Janet, went to return the book. Sip on this wine and enjoy the view until I get back. It's time for us to smell the roses again. Love, Robert"

Robert went back to the bedroom, quickly changed into a pair of shorts and sneakers, picked up the book and headed out the door. He whistled James Brown's song as he walked down the beach path toward the lighthouse and Professor Briggs' house. This was going to be the finest afternoon he and Janet have spent together in years.

CHAPTER 28

When Jonathon came to, he was sitting in the middle of one of the wooden chairs from his kitchen table. His arms were circled around the back of the chair and his hands were lashed with rope to the chair. His feet were also bound. Janet and Paul were strapped into the two leather easy chairs with duct tape. They were facing him. Paul's hand was also bandaged with duct tape. John Nguyen and Chien were busy rifling through drawers and cabinets in the house.

"I'll save you a lot of trouble," Jonathon said to them. "It's not in the house."

"Okay, then" John Nguyen said as he stopped his search and walked over to Jonathon. "Let's hope that fact doesn't cause you or your friends any trouble."

"So, Stuart, or what is it they call you here? Jonathon, where's the memory stick?"

"Rest assured it's in a safe place, and I'll deliver it to you after I make a deal with Uncle Bao."

John Nguyen laughed out loud. "Why would Uncle Bao want to make a fucking deal with you now?"

"Simple quid pro quo, I have something of value to him and he has something of value to me."

"Ah, but in this negotiation," John Nguyen said walking over to Paul and Janet, "I would say I have the upper hand." As he finished his sentence John Nguyen suddenly smashed his fist into Paul's wounded hand. Paul grimaced, but choked back any cry of pain.

John Nguyen continued, "The only fucking deal you are in a position to make is which one of your bullshit friends here you get to watch me kill first and whether it's slow and painful or swift and merciful."

"Again, unnecessary and unwise. You need my cooperation to get the memory stick back and you do not need to kill them to get my cooperation. I have no grudge against Uncle Bao. The information I took was my life insurance policy. I simply want to cash it in now and we all go our merry way."

"But you were an F.B.I. informant. You were going to turn over incriminating information to the F.B.I. Uncle Bao is not happy about that and you might have triggered a penalty clause in that damn life insurance policy of yours."

Janet watched in horror and amazement as the two men continued to nonchalantly discuss the terms of a deal that would determine whether she lived or died today.

"Uncle Bao knew I was an F.B.I. informant. In fact, as best as I can tell, he used it to his advantage whenever possible, sometimes leaking incorrect information down to me. He also knows that there is a balancing game that must be played with the F.B.I. Sometimes you give them something real to keep their confidence in their source. So, he would sacrifice a few of the lesser members of the organization from time to time; ones that didn't know enough or had strong enough family connections that he knew they wouldn't talk. I wasn't going to be one of them. I think Uncle Bao would respect that."

"I suppose he might have, but you didn't offer him the deal for the information, you offered it to the fucking F.B.I., didn't you?"

"The key there John is that I offered it. I offered it to buy myself some time, but I never gave it to them. Think about it. I could have easily turned it over before I was arrested, immediately after my arrest or after I escaped. I did none of those."

"Yeah, but what if you hadn't escaped. What would you have done then?"

"I can't say. Both sides put me in a difficult spot. I didn't have any good options. That's why I just disappeared and gave the information to no one."

"You see Jonathon, that's the problem with playing two ends against the middle, sometimes you run out of middle."

"So it appears, and when that happens you must choose one end or the other and I have chosen yours."

"Actually, I don't believe you had a fucking choice."

"Let's not argue over semantics."

John Nguyen paced back and forth in front of Jonathon. Chien stood behind Janet and Paul, his arms crossed in front of his chest, with the gun he was holding in his right hand resting on top. It was jarringly quiet. John Nguyen finally broke the silence.

"So, your part of the deal is that you take me to where the memory stick is and give it to me and in return, we spare your life. Is that it?"

"And the lives of my friends here."

"And how will I know that you won't go to the authorities with what you know after you hand over the stick?"

"There'd be no point. Without hard evidence, no one is going to take the word of an escaped petty criminal, especially one who has passed bad information to the F.B.I. before."

"And what guarantee do I have that you will lead us to the information and not into a fucking trap."

"First of all, I wasn't expecting you, so how could I have set up a trap? Second, you can leave my friends tied up here. If I double cross you, you can come back and kill them. If I don't, I'll come back and let them go."

Paul squirmed under his constraints. He had heard enough of this dispassionate discourse regarding their lives. "Briggs, you son of a bitch. You know you won't come back here. How dare you barter with our lives?"

Paul addressed his next comment to John Nguyen. "We have nothing to do with this business. Do what you want with him, but just let us go. We won't say anything about it. The sooner Briggs is gone from here, dead or alive, the better. No one will even question that he is gone."

John Nguyen spun around on his heels and looked at Paul. He gave a slight nod of his head to Chien. Chien calmly unfolded his arms, leaned forward and slapped Paul's face hard with the backside of his left hand.

"Shut the fuck up. No talking, unless I tell you to." John Nguyen scolded him like he was a child. He turned to Janet, "And you lady? What do you think?"

Janet was hesitant to speak. She looked over at Paul and then at Jonathon. John Nguyen patiently waited for her to respond. "I think you can trust him," she finally answered. Paul's face reddened beyond the site of the slap.

"Maybe you're right," John Nguyen turned back to face Jonathon as he spoke. "But trust, once broken, must be earned. So, Jonathon, earn back my trust by telling me exactly where the fuck the information is and how we can get it today."

Jonathon knew he had to tell the truth; or at least enough of it to get them to leave with him. It was his best chance for survival and Janet and Paul's only chance. Jonathon explained that he had deposited the memory stick, along with the encryption code, with a company called IT Keepsafe in San Francisco. He could retrieve it in person at any time with proper identification, but he had to give them at least two hours advance notice before picking it up.

"Is that it?" John Nguyen asked.

"Pretty much." Jonathon answered.

There was a perceptible fissure in John Nguyen's composed demeanor as he approached Jonathon. He grabbed him by the shoulders and shook him. "Do you think I'm a fucking idiot," he screamed.

He punched Jonathon in the abdomen. "We store documents in places like that too. You don't have to retrieve it in person. You can enter your account number and password online and they will deliver it to you within 24 hours." He punched Jonathon again. "What's the fucking password?"

Jonathon sucked in some air a few times before answering, "I lost the password. That's why I didn't mention that option. And you said you wanted it today. Going in person was the only way I could think of to accomplish that."

"Bullshit! How do you lose a password? You mean you forgot it. Maybe this will jog your memory, old man." John Nguyen jammed his knee into Jonathon's rib. Jonathon winced in pain and coughed.

"You can break all of my ribs and it won't help," Jonathon said with labored breathing. "I never memorize passwords. Carry-over from my days in Vietnam. I write a code that will give me the password when I need it."

"Where is the code written down?"

"That's what I lost. You see I change the password every so often and write a new code for it in some obscure place. Last time I changed the password, I wrote a code for it in a friend's book. That friend and the book are now gone." Jonathon stopped to catch his breath.

John Nguyen strolled over to Janet and bent down so that he was looking her directly in the eyes. "Do you believe that bullshit?"

"Yes," Janet said without hesitation.

"Why," he asked without taking his eyes off hers.

"Because, not too long ago, he told me the story of how he used code to send messages in Vietnam."

"And did he tell you about writing a code in a friend's book?"

"No."

John Nguyen stood up. "So, you can tell the truth. Good for you. Now, maybe you can help me get Jonathon to be more forthcoming."

He took the ka bar knife out of his pocket and cut the duct tape holding Janet's midsection to the chair. He left the tape around her shoulders and feet. He slid the knife seductively down her chest and around her breasts. He cut her blouse open.

"You have such a nice body. It would be a shame to see you lose a piece of it. Isn't that right Jonathon?"

"You can have the stick today. It's just a forty-minute drive from here. I can call them now. We don't need the code for the password. I ..."

There was knock on the door. Chien squatted behind Janet's chair and jabbed his gun into her back. John Nguyen slipped behind Jonathon and whispered, "You expecting company?"

Jonathon shook his head indicating that he was not.

"Okay, nobody move, no one is home," John Nguyen instructed. They waited in silence; each person frozen in place. There was another knock on the door, followed by a voice. It was Robert's.

"Hello, Professor Briggs, are you there? It's Robert Reed. I believe I have a book that belongs to you."

John Nguyen smiled when he heard Robert mention the book and cut the ropes that bound Jonathon's hands and feet together. He poked the knife in his back and walked him toward the door. "Answer it. No fucking around."

Jonathon cracked the door open, filling the opening with his body. "Hello, sorry, I was in the back of house, working on a project."

Robert handed him the book. "My wife left me a note. Said you needed this book returned as soon as possible."

"Yes, thank you. Very kind of you to bring it up here."

"I want to thank you for being so helpful to my wife with her research. This memorial idea means a lot to her, to us both."

"Happy to help. Well, listen, I hate to be rude, but I really do need to get back to my project. Thank you again." Jonathon closed the door.

John Nguyen pulled Jonathon away from the door and peaked furtively out the window as Robert walked down the path toward the lighthouse. When Robert was out of sight, he shepherded Jonathon back to his chair and retied his hands behind the chair.

"Is this the book?" he asked Jonathon, shoving the book in his face. "The book with the code?"

"No," Jonathon replied.

"You'd better not be shitting me." John Nguyen said as he flipped through the book. As Paul watched John Nguyen peruse the pages, he had an epiphany. He knew where the code was. Forget Jonathon, he was going to make his own deal.

"I think I know where the code is." Paul blurted out, willing to risk another blow. "If I can get you the code, will you let Janet and me go?"

John Nguyen threw the book on the floor and walked over to Paul. "You're not in the best fucking position to make a deal but, what the hell, tell me what you know."

"There's a notebook that belonged to a girl who died on the cliffs by the lighthouse about five months ago. Briggs knew her. The notebook was lost until just last week, when Janet found it. There are some titles written in Briggs' handwriting on the back cover. I didn't realize until just this moment that they might be a code for something."

"Where's the notebook?"

"It's in a backpack in my car."

Janet and Jonathon looked at each other, stunned. They both knew that Paul had just signed their death warrants.

CHAPTER 29

Robert sat down at the bench at the lighthouse before heading back to the cottage. He wanted to think. Something was bothering him about the exchange at Professor's Briggs house, but he couldn't quite put his finger on it. The conversation had been rather brief, but then, they didn't know each other, and he was a reclusive professor. Robert closed his eyes and replayed the conversation in his head.

It was his eyes; his eyes were tense. They didn't match the words he said. He was hiding something. Years of being at the negotiation table honed his ability to read those signs. But there was something else, something amorphous that he had sensed. That's what was really nagging at him. He took in a deep breath of fresh air, and then it dawned on him, Janet's perfume. He smelled the faint scent of Janet's perfume at Professor Brigg's house.

Robert dropped his head and covered his face with his hands as he put the pieces together. She's up there with Briggs. She didn't expect him back until tomorrow. Damn it! He knew she was in a vulnerable state. He knew she needed comforting. Why didn't he give it to her? Now she has turned to someone else. Maybe he's overreacting. Maybe she is just looking at some more of his books. But then, why didn't she say something when he was at the door? No, she was having an affair.

Robert kicked at the dirt in front of the bench. Why now? Why now, when he was ready to give her what she really needed? In the minutes that he sat there, Robert's emotions went from dejection to anger to determination. He would fight to get her back. He loved her and she loved him. He knew she did. He decided to go back up to the house and confront them.

Robert strode briskly up the path back to Professor Briggs' house. His original intention was to knock on the door and demand to talk to his wife. As he approached, however, he decided he had to see what was going on first and snuck around to the side of the house.

The first window Robert came to was next to a stack of firewood. Robert figured it was a living room window and would be a good place to steal a look. Warily, Robert raised his head until his eyes barely peered over the window sill. It took all his willpower not to cry out when he saw what was going on.

John Nguyen stood in front of Janet. He held the knife in one hand. "So, your name is Janet. You are the 'J' person who sent the fax with the picture. I should thank you. Without you, we would not have found your friend Jonathon."

Janet quickly glanced at Jonathon. He looked wounded. She looked down, not wanting to meet his eyes. John Nguyen lifted her chin with the knife. "Why didn't you tell me about the fucking notebook," he demanded and slapped her in the face with his other hand before she could answer. Janet remained silent.

"Don't think you can outsmart me, Janet. It's dangerous to your health." He slapped her again.

Paul cut in. "Stop. She didn't know the significance of the code either. Please, stop. I'll get you the book and then you can let us go." His last statement was void of any conviction. It sounded more like a whiny plea. Even Paul now realized that the chance that any of them would get out of this situation alive was negligible.

John Nguyen cut Paul's tape and jerked him out of the chair. He bent the thumb on Paul's good hand toward his wrist and twisted Paul's arm behind his back. "Chien, the pastor and I are going to go for a walk to his car. Keep your eye on these two. If they give you any trouble, inflict as much fucking pain as possible. But don't kill

182

them. We have a code to decipher when I return."

He turned to Jonathon. "We can do this the easy way, or the hard way. You fucking think about that until I get back." John Nguyen pressed the knife into Paul's back and shoved him toward the back door.

Robert ducked down behind the woodpile. His mind raced as he periodically peaked over the top of the stack at the two men walking away through the woods behind the house. He had to do something. He had to save Janet. The other guy in the house had a gun. He would have the element of surprise, but still, he needed some kind of weapon.

He looked around. A log would be too unwieldy. He spotted the wooden staff Jonathon kept along side the woodpile. That might work, it had a long reach. If he could sneak up on the armed man, he could crack him over the head and knock him out. Robert waited until the two men were out of sight, then he grabbed the stick and headed for the back door.

Chien circled around Jonathon's chair and then walked over and did the same to Janet's. He stopped and stood next to Janet. He was facing the front door. Jonathon was to his right. He pointed the gun that he held in his right hand at Jonathon, but kept his eyes trained on the opening in Janet's blouse. "You shouldn't make John Nguyen mad," he said to Janet. "He likes to cut things. Me, I like to touch."

He slipped his left hand inside her blouse and under her bra. Janet shifted around in the chair, trying to withdraw her breast from his grip. Chien smiled. "I like feisty women too."

Jonathon started to move forward in his chair. Chien cocked his gun, lowered it toward Jonathon's legs and warned. "You move again, I shoot off your kneecaps."

Chien turned his attention back to Janet. He leisurely slid his left hand down her midriff and over her belly until it came to rest on her jeans. He popped open the snap and slowly unzipped her pants.

Janet held her breath and stayed very still. She couldn't escape, so there was no use in fighting, especially if it was just going to give him more pleasure. She turned her head to the side, trying to bury it in the chair. That's when, out of the corner of her eye she spotted Robert, creeping inch by inch toward Chien, clutching a stick with both hands high over his head. He was less than fifteen feet away.

Janet turned back to face Chien, hoping to distract him from Robert's advance. "Please, don't," she pleaded. "I'm a married woman. I'm a mother." The moment Janet uttered those words, she burst into tears. She wasn't acting. All the events of the past week came flooding back to her. How did she go from an idea for a memorial for Daniel to this? All she wanted now was to go home with Robert.

Robert was almost within striking range when he stepped on a floorboard that creaked. Chien spun around and fired his gun in the direction of the sound. Robert slumped to the ground. Janet screamed.

Jonathon sprang up and thrust himself with the chair into Chien. The force of the blow crashed them both into the wall behind Janet, dislodging the gun from Chien's hand and breaking the chair apart. Jonathon jumped up. He was free of the chair, but his hands were still tangled with rope. He kicked the gun across the room, out of Chien's reach and disentangled his hands.

Chien pulled himself up along the wall and shook off his temporary daze. He grabbed a chair leg and threw it at Jonathon. Jonathon ducked and backed away from Chien. Chien grabbed another chair leg and lunged at Jonathon, swinging it like a club. Jonathon was able to fend off the first blow with another duck, followed by a counter offensive arm block to Chien's forearm. Chien spun around with a roundhouse kick and knocked Jonathon backwards to the floor.

Chien descended on Jonathon with a fury, landing a vicious blow to Jonathon's ribs with the chair leg. Jonathon squirmed backwards in pain as Chien raised the chair leg for another swing. He crashed it down on Jonathon's knee.

Jonathon felt his walking staff on the floor behind him and

brought it forward, just in time to block Chien's third hit. The block threw Chien off balance and Jonathon wasted no time. He reversed the direction of the staff, catching Chien between his legs and upended him. Jonathon sprang to his feet and, with one swift underhanded movement, rammed the spear end of his staff through Chien's neck. Chien went limp.

CHAPTER 30

Jonathon rushed over to Janet and ripped off her constraints. "Go get the gun in the corner," he ordered. Janet obediently ran to get the gun. Jonathon went over to Robert and felt for a pulse. "He's still alive."

As Jonathon tried to lift Robert up to a seated position, he grabbed his ribs and groaned. His knee was starting to throb. It was going to be difficult to put any extra weight on it. Chien inflicted more damage than he thought. He wasn't in any shape for a fight with John Nguyen right now.

"Janet, quickly, we have to get out of here. Grab the other side and help me lift him," he called out to her.

Robert moaned as they lifted him to his feet. With Robert draped between them, Janet and Jonathon made their way to the lighthouse. Janet took the tool from her pocket and handed it to Jonathon. He opened the door, and after they slipped in, immediately relocked it.

They leaned Robert against the wall. Jonathon instructed Janet to go fetch the crate behind the staircase and set it behind Robert for support. Jonathon examined Robert more closely. "If he had to get shot," he said to Janet, "he got shot in a fairly good place. It's an abdominal wound but it doesn't look like any major organs were hit. We do have to do something to stop the bleeding though."

Jonathon took off his shirt and tore it into long strips. Janet held Robert upright while Jonathon folded a few strips into a bandage and applied it to the wound. He had Janet hold the bandage in place while he wrapped another few strips tightly around Robert's waist to hold the bandage in place.

"It's probably best if we lay him down flat now," Jonathon said when he finished tying the strips.

They gently lowered Robert to the ground. Janet stroked his face. "I'm so sorry, Robert," Janet whispered as she bent over and kissed his forehead. Robert opened his eyes and smiled faintly at Janet before closing his eyes again. Tears silently rolled down her checks. "Don't die, Darling, please don't die. I couldn't bear to lose you too. I don't know what I'd do without you. I've been so stupid. Please, please, please, don't leave me." Janet buried her face in Robert's chest.

Jonathon gave her a moment with Robert. He slumped against the curved wall. His breathing was labored. After a few minutes, he spoke softly to Janet. "Janet, he'll be okay. We'll get him medical assistance soon. But right now, we must come up with a plan. It won't be hard for John Nguyen to figure out where we are."

Janet looked up at Jonathon. "You know I didn't mean for any of this to happen?"

"Neither did I. But why were you investigating me?"

"When I found Sarah's book, there was a poem in there about you. She had a hunch you were from New Orleans. That combined with the fact that Paul was so suspicious of you, led me to do a Google search of Jonathon Briggs. I found his obituary."

Jonathon leaned his head back against the wall. Janet continued. "Then, when I was sending a picture of Sarah's stepfather to a reporter friend of mine in Austin to try and help Charlene figure out what happened to him after Hurricane Katrina, I came across your picture in Paul's desk. It all sort of happened organically. I decided to see if he could find out who you were too."

"I see. And let me guess, the stepfather was in prison and your reporter friend found out I was also."

"Not exactly, he had a contact in the U.S. Marshall's service who… Wait a minute. I have his number in my pocket."

Janet reached down and searched Robert's pockets for his cell phone. He never went anywhere without it. She let out a deep sigh. Nothing. He must have changed in a hurry and left it in his work pants. She briefly wondered what was going on with Robert. He wasn't even supposed to be home before tomorrow and he rarely did errands for her, like returning the book.

"Was the agent you spoke to named Rick Sheffield?"

"Yes."

"Does he know you are here?"

"I'm not sure. My phone went dead after he told me those two weren't F.B.I. agents, like we thought. He knows I'm in this general area but not exactly where."

"At least that clears up one thing for me."

"What's that?"

"Rick Sheffield is not in cahoots with the Pham operative in the F.B.I."

"How did you ever get involved with the Pham family?"

"The other night, when I told you about Mai, I didn't tell you the whole story. The gambling lounge I met her in was run by the Pham organization. And she wasn't a regular employee, she was more like their slave.

She was smuggled into Vancouver illegally. Her family thought she could have a better life in North America. But the group that smuggled her in told her that her parents didn't pay enough, and she had to work for them for a while to pay them back. So, she worked in their gambling and prostitution parlors for a while and eventually was smuggled into Oklahoma with a shipment of ecstasy to the Pham organization.

After we fell in love, I offered to buy her out of her 'servitude'. I couldn't afford the price they were asking, so I offered to work for them myself in her place. Uncle Bao liked the fact that I was an Anglo who spoke Vietnamese and Khmer.

Most of his clients are Asian. He wanted me to eavesdrop on their conversations and report any information I discovered. He wanted to know who had money, who was trying to cheat, who might be affiliated with another gang or the police. Eventually, I worked my way up to running one of the lounges and getting a cut of the profits."

"And the F.B.I.?"

"About a year after I started working for the Pham organization, the F.B.I. started looking for someone to feed them information about their ecstasy operation. They found out about my background in Vietnam and thought I would be good. They also found out about Mai and threatened to deport her if I didn't cooperate. So, we made a deal."

Jonathon shifted his position on the wall, winced and coughed. "In the beginning, it worked out pretty well. I played one side against the other and managed to keep everyone at bay. I also profited nicely from both. I was saving up so Mai and I could go away somewhere."

"Why did you stay after Mai died?"

"It was all I had left. Besides, neither one was the kind of boss you could just call up and say, 'I quit.' So, when I saw a chance to create a new identity and get away from both of them, I took it." Jonathon coughed again and took in a few short painful breaths.

"Maybe it would help if you sat up straighter," Janet offered. "Here," she said reaching for the crate now sitting next to Robert, "why don't you try sitting against this."

Janet carried the crate over to Jonathon. He leaned forward and she arranged it behind his back. As she did so, she noticed a little tuft of matted hair on one corner. She drew her hand back.

"Great," she said sarcastically.

"What now?"

"It looks like there may be rats in here."

"Rats are the least of our worries. Let's figure out our next move. Where did you put the gun?"

"It's on the floor, over by Robert."

"Go get it. Do you know how to use it?"

"I've shot a .22 rifle before, shooting at cans at my grandparent's ranch, but never a hand gun."

"It's not that different. Bring the gun up to your eye level if that helps and remember to keep your arm steady and hold your breath when you squeeze the trigger. Okay, now, I want you to take the gun and climb up to the watch room. Sneak a look out the window to see if you can spot John Nguyen. Stay low though, we don't want him to see you."

"Do you want me to try and shoot at him if I see him?"

"No, the range will be too far for any kind of accuracy. The gun is for when he gets inside the lighthouse. You best get going."

Janet climbed up the stairs as far as she could, then turned and looked dolefully back at Robert and Jonathon. "Go on, hurry," Jonathon urged. Janet climbed up on the railing and hauled herself up to the watch room just as she had the day she found Sarah's notebook. She crawled over to a window and cautiously glimpsed out from the bottom corner.

"Oh no," she shouted down to Jonathon. "He's coming out of the woods. He has Paul in front of him. He's pointing a gun at Paul's head. Paul looks hurt."

Paul took the brunt of John Nguyen's fury when they returned to find Chien dead and Janet and Jonathon gone. His nose was broken and his mouth was bleeding. His right arm dangled limp at his side.

"What's he doing now," Jonathon called up to Janet.

"He's looking around. Wait, now he's heading toward the lighthouse."

"I figured he would. We left a good trail with Robert's blood and our footprints. Janet, listen to me very carefully. At some point, he is going to break down the door. I want you to lie down on the floor near the corner of the opening to the watch room and take aim at the door. When he first enters, it will take a few moments for his eyes to adjust to the dimmer light in here. You will have a few seconds advantage to get a good shot off at him."

"I've never shot anybody before. What if I can't do it? You should shoot at him."

"You can do it. You have to. I don't know how steady my aim will be right now. Besides, you have the best vantage point from up there. Aim for his head or the arm that is holding the gun, whichever you have a better shot at."

"Okay, okay, I'll try."

"Janet, don't hesitate. You need to shoot at him right away while his eyes are adjusting. Be prepared, he'll probably be using Paul to shield his body, I'll pull Paul away when they enter."

Jonathon smashed the crate against the wall with his left arm. He tapped Robert's arm. "Still with us pal?" Robert opened his eyes and shook his head. "It may get rough in here in a few minutes. Hold on to this," Jonathon said as he wrapped Robert's hand around one of the pieces of broken board. Jonathon grabbed a few shards of board for himself, stood up and slowly limped along the rock wall until he was next to the door.

Janet looked down at the two wounded men preparing for battle. She never asked Jonathon what she should do if he couldn't pull Paul out of the way. She already knew the answer. Janet took a few deep breaths, positioned herself on the floor, and took aim at the lighthouse door.

CHAPTER 31

John Nguyen stopped a few feet in front of the lighthouse door. He held Paul between him and the door with a gun still pointed at Paul's head. "Stuart," he called out, "That was not a fucking nice thing that you did to my friend Chien. What'd he do, screw the girl? He had a bad habit that way. I told him it would get him fucking killed one day.

Looks like it was a good fight, though. From the trail of blood, one of you must be pretty fucked up. The sooner I get the password, the sooner you can get medical assistance. Open the door. Let's finish this up."

No one inside the lighthouse made a sound. Janet's heart was pounding as she kept her focus on the door. John Nguyen continued to shout at them through the door. "I know you are fucking in there. Pastor Paul here, has the blue notebook with the code. He can't decode it. I'm sure of that, now. But he does know the bible verse, in case you forgot that.

I even found the poem named in the notebook in that damn book that was dropped off. Brought the pages to you. I'm trying to make this fucking easy for you, Stuart. Open the door and tell me what I need to know, and this can all be over."

Again, everyone inside the lighthouse remained silent. Janet and Robert were following Jonathon's lead. Jonathon was glad that John Nguyen thought he needed the actual bible verse to decipher the code and not just the numbers. It would keep Paul alive, at least for now.

John Nguyen's tone sharpened. "Open the door or you and all of your fucking friends will be very sorry." He squeezed Paul's mangled arm. Paul cried out in pain. Jonathon flinched, but still did not say a word. Janet's hands started shaking. She lowered the gun down for a minute and tried taking some yoga breaths to steady her nerves; inhaling slowly through her nose and exhaling slowly out of her mouth with pursed lips.

John Nguyen pushed Paul over to the door. "Kick the God Damn door in," he commanded. Paul kicked forcefully at the door, but it did not budge. "Kick harder," John Nguyen yelled at him, clenching his broken arm again, "or I'll start breaking some of your other fucking bones."

Paul let out a guttural yell as he thrust at the door again. It still didn't open. John Nguyen grabbed the wrist on Paul's broken arm and started twisting it. "Wait," Paul screamed. "Wait, I think I might have a key for that door. Look on my keychain. It has a square head and is a little thicker than the others."

John Nguyen released Paul's wrist and reached into his pocket with his left hand for the keys. His right hand pressed the gun firmly against Paul's back. He jingled the keys around until he found a square one. He slipped it into Paul's good hand and instructed him to unlock the door and slowly open it.

John Nguyen moved in close behind Paul, raising the gun to the back of Paul's head. As they heard the key turn in the lock, Janet, Jonathon and Robert readied themselves for what was about to happen, even though none of them had any idea exactly what that was going to be.

As Paul swung the door open, Jonathon hugged his body against the wall, trying to stay hidden by the side of the door. Paul and John Nguyen stepped into the threshold as one form. Janet could make out Paul's outline clearly, but very little of John Nguyen was visible. Janet knew she only had seconds left to get any advantage. Please Jonathon, she thought, do something.

She focused harder on the form. Then she saw a corner of a man's head behind Paul. She knew she could never shoot that precisely. God, what was she going to do? Janet held her breath. She imagined pulling the trigger. She visualized the bullet traveling in a perfect line, hitting her target squarely in the middle, just like her grandfather taught her years ago.

Suddenly, Jonathon reached out from behind the door and pulled at Paul's arm. Janet squeezed the trigger. John Nguyen's gun also discharged as he hit the floor and rolled into the room. Paul tumbled to the floor. John Nguyen spun onto on his back, reached up with his gun and discharged it repeatedly into the wooden floor of the watch room.

Jonathon vaulted over Paul's body, landing a full contact body slam on John Nguyen. With both hands, Jonathon gripped John Nguyen's gun hand and smashed it against the floor until the gun fell out of his hand. John Nguyen wrapped his legs around Jonathon's middle and squeezed. Jonathon felt one of his cracked ribs snap. He gritted his teeth, and while still holding onto John Nguyen's wrist with one hand, he swung the other elbow back at John Nguyen's head. It was a solid connection.

John Nguyen grunted but did not release his leg hold on Jonathon's middle. He squeezed Jonathon harder. Jonathon wheezed and started to cough up blood. He could barely breathe.

Jonathon struck again at John Nguyen's head. His elbow slipped off the side of his head. It was wet. He was bleeding. Either he hit his head on the floor when Jonathon slammed into him or Janet grazed his head with her shot. Janet was the last thing Jonathon thought of before he passed out.

CHAPTER 32

Ever since 9/11, one of the perks of being a U.S. Marshall was that you could catch a free ride on any commercial airliner with an open seat. Rick Sheffield tried to calculate his odds of catching a flight to San Francisco any time soon as he sped toward the airport. It wasn't so much that he worried about finding a flight with an open seat; after all he could always commandeer a seat since this was for official business. No, it was whether there would be a flight that would get him anywhere near Half Moon Bay leaving from Oklahoma City in the middle of the day. The odds were not in his favor. Will Rogers Airport was not a hub for any major airline. He'd have a better chance of getting to the Bay area if he hopped a quick flight to Dallas first, but that would just eat up time he didn't have to spare.

He sighed and flipped open his cell phone. He'd better call Scratch. Rick hesitated for another second before he dialed the number. He knew Scratch would fly him to Half Moon Bay to pick up Wells if he asked him; it's just that Scratch Deavers was not the sort of man you wanted to have on the deficit side of your favor scale. You never knew exactly what the payback would entail.

"Hey Scratch. It's Rick."

"Rickster, what's up? Oh, sorry, I mean Marshall Rickster, what's up? Long time no hear." Rick had known Scratch since high school.

"You available to fly right now? I need a lift to the Bay area, and I don't have time to wait on a commercial flight."

"Is this official business?"

"Yes."

"Is it a paying gig?"

"Ha! I don't have a chance in hell of getting a requisition approved for your corporate gouging Lear prices, but if I bring in the guy I'm going after, I can probably get the Department to cover your gas, maybe a little more."

"Are you going after a bad ass? Maybe I could lend a little muscle. I haven't had much excitement lately."

"Somehow Scratch, I doubt that."

Ever since Rick had known Scratch, excitement, or more specifically trouble, seemed to follow Scratch like a new puppy. Yet somehow, he always came away with barely a scratch. Of course, that's not how he got his nickname; that came about from his locker room habit. But it did help to make the name stick. The name became permanent during his days in the Air Force when he flew the most dangerous missions in the Gulf War, always returning unscathed, but with plenty of near miss stories.

After his tour was over, Scratch came back to Tinker Air Force base and trained new pilots. That is until ranchers from Oklahoma, Texas and Colorado started reporting that low flying Air Force jets were strafing their cattle. Scratch was restricted to the classroom after that and resigned at the end of his second hitch.

Somehow Scratch was able to scrape together enough for a down payment on a used Lear jet and has been in business for himself ever since. He did pretty well for himself too. He had a few regular corporate clients and then took whatever other business turned up. Word on the street was that Scratch wasn't too particular about his clientele or their destination. He had a don't ask, don't tell policy if he got cash up front. Rick had used that same policy with Scratch for years, out of respect for their friendship.

"Can't tell you much about the guy except that he is a fugitive and may have put a woman reporter in grave danger."

"Rickster you sly dog, you're trying to rescue a damsel in distress! Okay buddy I'll do it. You can owe me a "Get out of jail free" card later. What's the destination?"

"Half Moon Bay."

"Okay, I'll program the nav system, file the flight plan, and start the preflight."

"Great, thanks Scratch. Be there in ten."

Rick hung up the phone, put on his flasher and sped to the private airstrip where Scratch kept his plane. He began to formulate his plan of action in his head as he drove. What was it Janet was saying when she was cut off? He lives in a house behind a lighthouse north of …. North of what? Half Moon Bay? Pescadaro Park? Somewhere in between? Rick called his office and asked his secretary to run a google search on lighthouses along the California coast from Half Moon Bay to Pescadaro Creek Park.

While he waited, Rick wondered if Janet was alright. He hoped she had stayed put like he told her too. From the brief conversation he had with her, he got the feeling that she wasn't the kind of gal who could sit tight very long. Reporters in general were bad about that, female reporters were the worst. If his gut feeling was right, she'd gone straight to Wells to warn him. But he'd better ask his secretary to call the local sheriff's office and have them run by Pescadaro Creek Park now to check just in case.

Rick's secretary came back on the line and reported that two lighthouses came up in the search, one north of Half Moon Bay and one north of Pescadaro. Great, Rick thought, that's not much help. Maybe he should call the U.S. Marshall's office in San Francisco and have them send a team to each lighthouse.

No, he'd better play this one close to his chest. He couldn't risk a tip off, or worse another leak, when he was this close. He'd call the local police and ask them to have a car ready to pick him up at Half Moon

Bay. They could take him to whichever lighthouse he decides Wells most likely lives behind. His only worry now was could he pick the right one and get there in time?

He pulled into Scratch's hanger, threw his car into park and boarded the plane.

"Okay Scratch, show me what this baby can do."

CHAPTER 33

Janet rolled up against the wall when John Nguyen started shooting at the watch room floor. One bullet grazed the sole of her shoe, but otherwise she was unharmed. She was too petrified to scream. When she heard the scuffle start below, she crawled back out to the staircase opening. She trained the gun on the two men but could not find a clear shot at John Nguyen.

After Jonathon collapsed on top of John Nguyen, Janet watched as he disengaged his legs and flipped Jonathon over in front of himself to use as a shield. John Nguyen pulled Jonathon along with him by his shirt collar as he inched along the floor toward his gun.

As John Nguyen reached out for his gun, his arm was exposed and part of his head and shoulder stretched out beyond Jonathon. Janet knew this might be her last chance. She held her breath and fired another shot. She hit him in the shoulder.

"Fucking Shit!" John Nguyen yelled. He pulled himself back beneath Jonathon and swung them both hard so they were leaning against the wall. He briefly released his grip from Jonathon's collar and grabbed a knife from his belt. He held the knife across Jonathon's neck. "Stop shooting or I slit his throat."

Janet pulled the gun in toward her chest and rolled back against the wall. She wished she were a better shot. The room was quiet.

"Good Janet," John Nguyen called out, "Now, I want you to toss the gun gently down on the staircase and climb down."

Janet tried to evaluate the situation rationally in her mind. She was safe up here for now and could shoot John Nguyen if he tried to climb up. But Robert was going to bleed to death if he didn't get help soon. She didn't know if Paul was dead or not and Jonathon was unconscious, probably with a collapsed lung, with a knife at his throat.

Emotion crept in. God, what should she do? This was all her fault. If they died, what did she have to live for? They can't save themselves. She had to try to save them.

"Janet," John Nguyen called out again, "Don't make me kill them."

"Okay," Janet yelled back. "I'm coming down."

Janet got up and walked over to the opening by the staircase. She still held the gun, but it was hanging at her side. Paul started to stir as she looked at the men below. He pushed himself up with his left arm and leaned back against the wall.

Paul felt dizzy. He reached over with his left hand and felt the right side of his head. It was bleeding and part of his ear was missing, but it didn't feel like the bullet had entered his skull. Paul didn't know whether to thank or kill Briggs for the little stunt he and Janet just pulled. He looked over at John Nguyen and Jonathon. It didn't look like it was going to matter anyway.

"Throw the gun down first," John Nguyen instructed, "put the safety on and then toss it down on the stairs."

"No Janet," Robert cried out as he tried to sit up. "Save yourself," he continued before he crumpled back to the floor.

John Nguyen looked across the room at Robert. He recognized him as the man who brought the book back. He must have come back, and surprised Chien. Looks like Chien got the best of him. He looked back up at Janet. "Three men, Janet. You are a popular girl. They will all die if you do not do as I say. Now, toss down the gun."

Janet flipped the safety on the gun, leaned over the edge of the opening and dropped the gun onto the staircase. It landed in the middle of the staircase. John Nguyen stood up, dragged Jonathon over by Paul and deposited him against the wall. "Wake the asshole up," he commanded Paul. "You two have some decoding to do."

He walked up the staircase, tucked the knife back in his belt and picked up the gun. He sat down sideways on the steps. From that position, he could see Janet at the edge of the watch room, Paul and Jonathon against the wall at the bottom of the staircase, and Robert lying down against the far wall. He pointed the gun at Paul and Jonathon, then glanced up at Janet and motioned to her with his head to come down. "Come on, climb down and join the fucking party."

"I can't climb down. I sort of have to jump down."

"So, jump down. Just don't fucking land near me or I'll shoot your ass."

Janet jumped toward the staircase with her arms outstretched, catching the railing and swinging over the top, just as she had last Sunday. This time though, she didn't get her legs hooked onto the railing and crashed into the top of the staircase. The force of the crash pushed her body back and she found herself hanging from the railing.

Janet struggled to maintain her grip. She looked down at the floor below her. She could see the dusty outline of the spot where the crate used to be. It was a long way down.

John Nguyen watched her but offered no help. He seemed amused at her predicament. Janet started swinging her legs until she had enough momentum to reach the stairs. She had to carefully gauge when to land with her feet and let go of her hands. She was losing strength in her arms so she would have to do it soon.

Janet counted to three to herself and with one final push, swung her legs up, arched her back and released her hands. She came down in the middle of the staircase several steps above John Nguyen and steadied herself with the rail on the opposite side. She still had not formulated a plan.

"Impressive," he said to her. "Now get the fuck over here." Janet followed his orders and walked down the steps to John Nguyen. He stood as she approached and when she reached him, he shoved her and sent her flying down the stairs. Janet landed on the floor in front of Paul and Jonathon.

John Nguyen pointed his gun at the two men as he walked down the stairs to Janet. He furiously kicked at her body as she lay sprawled out on the floor. Janet buried her head in her arms and curled into a ball.

"You, Bitch," John Nguyen screamed, as he kept kicking her. "I told you not to fuck with me." Then he stopped, sat down on the bottom step and leaned against the rail. Janet didn't move. She didn't make a sound.

"Get up," he commanded her. "GET THE FUCK UP NOW and sit over here." He motioned to the bottom step. Janet looked up. She tried to push herself up to stand. She couldn't; her body was racked with pain. She crawled over to the bottom step and pulled herself up. She leaned against the railing opposite John Nguyen. Blood dribbled out of the corner of her mouth.

When she looked over at him, he said, "That was just a warm-up Janet, in case you have any other bright ideas brewing." His gaze turned in the direction his gun was pointing. "If you make one move, I will shoot them and then I will make you beg me to kill you too."

Paul managed to rouse Jonathon who was now alternately coughing and gasping for air. John Nguyen regained his composure.

"Okay gentlemen. No more fucking games. You have three minutes to get me the password. Pastor, give him the notebook." Paul crawled over to the base of the stairs where the notebook landed when he fell earlier. He cast a brief mournful look at Janet as he retrieved it. John Nguyen caught the glance.

Paul brought the notebook back to Jonathon and pulled the torn pages containing the poem out of his pocket. He spread the pages out in front of Jonathon who started studying the poem and the back page of the notebook.

"You'd better give me the fucking right one Stuart. I'm going to take Janet with me to your computer and if it doesn't work, she will die a slow and painful death." Jonathon didn't say a word. He kept looking back and forth between the clues in the notebook and the poem, concentrating on figuring out the password.

John Nguyen turned to Janet. "So, Janet, I guess you heard the good news; you get to be my hostage for a while longer. The bad news is that I'm going to have to kill one of these other bastards, so that your friend Jonathon over there will take his work and me seriously. Tell you what though, I will let you pick which one I kill."

The blood rushed out of Janet's face. "No, please," she pleaded. "You don't have to kill anyone. Jonathon will give you the right password. I won't give you any trouble, I promise."

"I believe you, but, after everything that's happened, I do need to kill someone. So, who will it be? Your camping buddy Pastor or your book loving friend over there," he said pointing to Robert.

"I can't. I can't. Please don't do this." Her eyes welled with tears as she spoke.

"If you don't choose, Janet, I will kill them both. So, who is it, Pastor Paul," John Nguyen looked over at Robert, "or..., what is his name?"

"Robert," Janet answered softly.

"or Robert, who is Robert, anyway?"

Before Janet could answer, Robert raised himself up on his elbow and tried to talk. His voice was weak. They couldn't hear him. He motioned for them to come over and lay back down.

"I don't know Janet, but if I was you, I'd pick Robert. It doesn't look like he's going to last much longer anyway. On the other hand, he's the better man if he's trying to volunteer to make this easier for you. Shall we go see what he has to say?"

John Nguyen motioned for Janet to get up and pushed her forward, toward Robert. He kept his eyes and gun on Paul and Jonathon as they walked over to Robert. When they reached Robert, Janet tried to kneel beside him, but John Nguyen held her back. "He will talk to me, not you," he said gruffly.

Tears streamed down Janet's face as she looked at Robert. When their eyes met, she tried to put on a brave face and smile through the tears. "I love you," Janet mouthed to him. His eyes conveyed the same silent message back to her.

John Nguyen moved closer to Robert, pushing Janet to one side and leaned down to hear what Robert had to say. Robert took in a few short breaths to gather some strength and then sat up suddenly with a tremendous burst of energy, plunging the wooden shank he held in his hand up through John Nguyen's ribcage into his heart.

Janet jerked herself away from John Nguyen's reach as he gasped and stumbled backwards. He fell back against the outside of the spiral staircase, dropping the gun. He made one desperate attempt to pull the stake out before he toppled to the floor. "I'm her husband," Robert said before collapsing.

CHAPTER 34

Janet rushed to Robert's side. She laid her head on his chest and wrapped her arms around his neck. "Robert," she sobbed softly, "Oh Robert." He didn't move. She raised her head up and looked at his face to see if she could see any sign that he was breathing. She couldn't tell from looking at him. She pressed her fingers against a vein in his neck. She thought she detected a faint pulse.

Janet gently kissed his lips. "I'll be back, Sweetheart. You hang on, I'm going to get help." Just as Janet started to stand up to go, she heard the shot. She whirled around and saw Paul standing over John Nguyen with the gun pointed at his head. John Nguyen lay in a pool of blood. Paul turned and pointed the gun at Jonathon.

"Paul," Janet screamed. "What are you doing? Put the gun down."

"I'm not taking any chances."

"Paul, Jonathon isn't one of them. He tried to help us."

"How can you say that? Look at us! This is all his doing."

"No," Janet said as she slowly inched over toward Jonathon. "It's my fault. I started the chain in motion. I put us in danger." Janet was now standing between Jonathon and Paul.

"No, it wasn't your fault; you didn't know. He shouldn't have come here. He put the whole community in danger. And, what about

Sarah? Have you forgotten what he did to her?"

Jonathon pushed himself up against the wall to his feet, but that exertion left him struggling to breathe. "Move Janet," was all he could manage to say. Janet ignored his command and kept talking to Paul.

"No, Paul, I haven't forgotten. We decided to let the police sort it out remember. Look, we need to get some medical help. Let's go together, just you and me, and find help."

"He'll run. I'm not going to let him get away."

"We'll lock him in. You have a key remember."

"So does he."

"I'll take his key. I'll take it right now."

Janet glanced back over her shoulder at Jonathon and then looked back at Paul. She cautiously stepped backwards toward Jonathon. She reached back without taking her eyes off Paul and reached into his pocket for the key tool.

"No," Paul yelled. "Leave it." Jonathon pressed something into Janet's hand when she reached behind her back toward his pocket. It was another one of the wooden shards from the crate. Janet took a breath and swallowed. She wasn't sure she could use it on Paul, but there was a certain comfort in having it handy.

She ran her hand down the stick. The sharp end was pointed down. She moved her hand back up to the top. She felt something fuzzy. It was the clump of hair she felt earlier. As she held it tight in her palm now, she decided that it was too long to be rat hair.

Janet looked past Paul to the space where the crate used to be and then traced an invisible line up to the top of the staircase. She imagined Sarah writing in her notebook in the watch room. When did she leave the notebook there? She remembered Jonathon's story about the rainy day. It couldn't have been that day. She wrote a poem about her chat with Jonathon after that day. No, Sarah came back. She knew where the county left the key. A sudden wave of nausea overtook her as the bits of information about Sarah suddenly came together in her mind.

"Janet, move away from him," Paul shouted, "He's going to use you as a hostage."

"No. No he won't…"

"Quit defending him, damn it!"

"Paul. How did you get a key to the lighthouse?"

"Janet, move now. I can still save you."

"It was the key the county hid, wasn't it? Sarah knew where it was. You met her up here the day she died, didn't you?"

Paul's eyes grew wide. His face reddened. Janet continued.

"She opened the lighthouse and was waiting for you in the watch room. You were the one she loved. P.B. – Paul Barnett, not Professor Briggs. You thought you were going to have another rendezvous with her. When you got here you helped her climb down. You started kissing her on the steps, but she stopped you. She was excited. Had news for you. News you didn't like.

You wanted her to have an abortion. She wanted to have the baby, your baby. You got angry and pushed her off the stairs. She hit her head on the crate, didn't she? You took the key from her pocket and locked her inside, until you figured out what to do."

"No, Janet, that's crazy…"

Janet seethed with anger and disgust for Paul. Sarah trusted him. Hell, she trusted him. But Sarah was young and vulnerable. She was just stupid. How could she be so blind? When she thought about what they were going to do on the camping trip, she cringed. Janet kept talking, cutting Paul off, her voice getting louder with each word.

"How convenient for you when Charlene called later that evening and told you Sarah was missing. You told Charlene you would come up here to look for her. In the dark, you took Sarah from the lighthouse and threw her over the cliff so it would look like an accident. You locked the lighthouse back up and walked around the area in a fake search, so when the police came they wouldn't question your footprints everywhere. Then you went to sit with Charlene.

How could you be so brazen, so cold? To sit and console the mother of the girl you just killed! You didn't call the police for hours so that the waves would smash her against the rocks enough times to cover any trace of the original fall, maybe lose evidence of the pregnancy. The police never searched the lighthouse because they didn't think that Sarah or anyone else had access to it. You kept the key to make sure it stayed that way. You didn't know she left the notebook in the watch room. You didn't know the evidence it contained."

"No, Janet. It was Briggs. He has a key. He did it."

"Stop it Paul, that doesn't make sense. You have the key that Sarah used to get in. And why didn't anyone see the autopsy, not even Charlene? She told me you handled it. You knew what it said. When I showed it to you earlier, you weren't upset about what it said; you were upset that I got a copy of it. And when you saw the notebook, you were so quick to try and convince me that Jonathon was her lover and her killer.

You lied to me. You tried to use me to frame an innocent man. And Sarah, how could you? She came to you for help. You didn't just fail Sarah; you took advantage of her and then you killed her!"

Janet stared at Paul. His mangled right arm was dangling limp by his side. His nose was broken and dried blood had matted the hair over where his ear used to be. He was taking short, rapid breaths. His eyes were bulging and wild. Paul looked like a cornered animal.

"I didn't kill her," he screamed at Janet. His left hand with the gun started shaking. Janet stepped back, pressing herself against Jonathon and the wall. Paul lowered his voice. His face and shoulders dropped. "She fell. It was an accident. I got angry when she told me she was pregnant, but I didn't touch her. She got scared, backed up and fell off the stairs. I tried to catch her. I tried to catch her..."

"Why didn't you just tell the police that?" Janet said softly.

"What was the point? She was already dead. If word got out that we..., that I... impregnated her, my career would have been over. I worked so hard for so many years. It was an accident, a horrible accident. I just changed the location to save her reputation and mine. I cared for her. I really did. Janet you have to believe me."

"I believe you, I do," Janet said to Paul in the soothing tone she used to use to calm Daniel down after a temper tantrum when he was little. "Put the gun down, Paul. Let's go get help."

"It's too late for that now." Paul spoke feverishly. "Janet, come to me. Stand by me. Briggs is going to die anyway. That crime organization will send more men after him. He'll put more people in danger. We can solve two problems now. We can say the hit man killed him, and any questions about Sarah's death can die with him. We can go off somewhere. Start fresh, just you and me."

Jonathon nudged Janet from behind to move to one side. "Let me take him," he whispered to her. She glanced back over her shoulder at him. He held a wooden shard in his hand, like the one she still had in hers. Janet's eyes filled with tears as she looked at him. She shook her head back and forth. "No," she mouthed to him. "I will."

Janet looked over at Robert lying on the floor. Teardrops silently rolled down her cheeks as she turned her focus back to Paul. She looked him in the eyes as she started taking baby steps toward him, keeping her body directly in front of the gun. Janet felt as if she were in a dream. Everything in the lighthouse except for Paul faded from view. Her movements felt exaggerated and slow.

"Paul," she said gently as she approached. "I already have a husband. I'm going with him." In that moment, Janet realized that she was not going to strike at Paul. She dropped the stake and reached both hands out toward the gun. She would either take the gun from Paul or she and Robert would join Daniel together. They would be a family again one way or the other.

Janet felt a wave of warmth wash over her as she relaxed and continued walking toward the gun. "Paul give me the gun. It's over."

Paul's eyes grew wide as he glimpsed at the stake on the floor. His shoulders snapped back to attention. He took a step sideways. Janet followed his lead. "Janet, get out of the way!"

Janet continued her unhurried, deliberate march toward the gun. "It's too late for that now," she stated plainly.

"Janet, Stop! Don't make me shoot you!" Paul clenched his jaw, his eyes narrowed. It was same angry face Janet had seen on Paul before. This time, though it didn't bother her. She locked eyes with him and kept walking forward.

"Damn it," he screamed. His eyes narrowed further, and his brow furrowed as he raised the gun slightly, aiming it directly at her heart.

Jonathon lunged forward crying out like a warrior in the heat of battle. The sound of the single gunshot reverberated throughout the lighthouse. Time and space were momentarily suspended. Janet clutched her chest and watched as Paul slumped to the floor.

"U.S. Marshall," a voice declared from the doorway to the lighthouse. "Everyone just stay where you are." Rick Sheffield, Scratch, and a local police officer quickly swept the room, collecting weapons and assessing the bodies. Rick walked over to Janet. "Ms. Reed, are you okay?" Janet nodded her head, not yet able to find her voice.

"Call the hospital and get a chopper out here," Marshall Sheffield instructed the officer. "We have a fella here who needs to get to the emergency room stat." He looked over at Jonathon.
"Wells, I see you managed to survive again."

"Took you long enough to find me." Jonathon said between breaths.

"You have no idea. But don't worry; you're going to be seeing a lot of me from now on."

Rick turned back to Janet. "Thanks for the call. You didn't make it very easy for me, but you gave me enough."

"I think I should be the one doing the thanking," Janet said, finally able to speak. "I should have heeded your warning."

"Well, if we all always do what we should do, the world would be a boring place." Scratch said, exchanging a grin with Rick. "Besides little lady, looks like you did all the hard work before Marshall Rick here showed up."

The helicopter ambulance arrived, and Robert was quickly loaded on board. Janet watched anxiously as the helicopter took off for the hospital. Jonathon and Rick stood beside her. Jonathon was in handcuffs.

Rick draped his coat over her shoulders. "Come on," he said "I'll drive you to the hospital. Looks like Wells needs some medical attention as well. You can give me your statements there."

As they turned to head down the path to the road, Janet stopped. "Wait, I forgot something in the lighthouse." She ran back inside and grabbed Sarah's notebook.

CHAPTER 35

Janet sat down on Sarah's bench at the lighthouse cliff. The sun was shining, and the wind was the calmest Janet had felt it in the two weeks since she first discovered this spot. She rubbed her hand over the dedication plaque. Janet thought about Sarah and the notebook.

Turning the notebook over to Charlene was the hardest thing she had to do. Not just because of what she had to explain to Charlene, but because she had grown close to Sarah through her writings and quest for the truth about her death. She wished she could have met Sarah. She hoped Daniel had.

Charlene took the news better than Janet expected her to. Of course, there was some anger and some tears, but at least she had closure. And more importantly to Charlene, Sarah didn't commit suicide. Charlene took great comfort in knowing that Sarah was now most certainly in heaven with the Lord, awaiting her arrival some day.

Janet also told her about Dewayne Williams' fate. And although Charlene expressed relief, there was a glint of sadness in her eyes. "Such a shame," she had told Janet, shaking her head. "He could be a good man when he tried."

"Yes," Janet had replied solemnly. "Even good men make mistakes, and sometimes, there's just no way to make things right again."

Janet thought about Paul. His parents had his body flown to Sacramento for burial, but the church had a memorial service for him yesterday. Janet didn't attend. She couldn't bring herself to go. Janet was astounded when Charlene stopped by the hospital to tell her that she had attended the service. "I had to go," she told Janet. "I had to forgive him. It's what the Lord would do. It's what Sarah would want."

Since Janet met her, Janet envied the strength Charlene got from her faith. But now, she feared that maybe Charlene might be using her faith to avoid dealing with her emotions. Then again, Charlene seemed at peace. And who was she to question someone's faith? She'd lost faith in her marriage and in her husband and she had been wrong.

Janet had been spending all her days and nights at the hospital with Robert. Other than her initial visit with Charlene, she only left the hospital that first night, when Robert was in recovery after surgery. She went back to the cottage to shower and change clothes. Rick Sheffield sent an officer with her. She found the flowers and Robert's note on the dining room table. She sobbed that night in the shower, like she never had before, not even after Daniel died.

Janet brought the flowers back with her to the hospital. She also brought the stone she found on the beach that first day. Though it was only two weeks ago, it seemed like a lifetime. She placed them both on the window sill in Robert's room. When he awoke and saw them, he smiled faintly. Janet kissed him on his forehead. He raised his hand and caressed her face.

"I'm sorry," he mumbled.

Janet placed a finger on his lips. "Shhh, don't talk. You don't need to."

Robert slid his hand down her cheek to his face and removed her finger from his lips. He clutched her hand to his heart. "Yes, I do," Robert paused and took a breath before he continued. "I was going to tell you this when I got home, before… you know. Reed men don't leave their women behind. I told that to Daniel once. But I did, Janet, didn't I, too many times. I wasn't there when you needed me."

Janet leaned over and pressed her lips tenderly against his. She squeezed his hand, "Robert, you were there when I needed you the most. Sleep now, my love." Robert drifted off to sleep. Janet slept in the chair by his bed. Over the next few days, when Robert was awake, they talked, they really talked.

"I thought I would find you here," a voice jarred Janet from her thoughts. Janet looked over her shoulder and saw Jonathon approaching the bench. Standing ten yards behind him, with his arms folded across his chest, Rick Sheffield observed.

"Jonathon…, I mean Stuart…," Janet said with surprise. She had not seen Jonathon since the ride over to the hospital last week.

"It's good to see you. I wasn't sure I would get the chance before I left. I tried to see you in the hospital after Robert was stable, but the nurses said you'd been released. They didn't tell me where you went."

Jonathon sat down next to her on the bench. "Our Marshall friend over there," Jonathon said motioning behind him with a nod of his head. "Turns out to be a vigilant watchdog and a pretty shrewd negotiator. He let me recuperate a few days in an innocuous motel and then took me for a drive to San Francisco.

It seems the price for a final farewell visit with you was the memory stick, and of course my agreement to testify against the Pham family. But first we are working on setting a trap for Jim Fletcher. We're both convinced that he's the Pham's F.B.I. operative."

"Well, I'm flattered that you used your 'insurance proceeds' to see me, but are you sure that's the best deal for you?"

Jonathon turned toward her and took her hands in his "Yes, my dear, it is." He gazed at her face and smiled. "Besides, it's time I stopped running from my past and pay the piper. Sheffield is a decent guy. He knows what he's doing. If it all works out as planned, I'll get to start over somewhere."

"Will I ever see you again?"

"I don't think so. I'm in protective custody until after the trial and then I'll be in the witness protection program – new town, new identity. It wouldn't be safe for me or you if I contact you."

"So, this is goodbye, then."

"I'm afraid so."

Jonathon stood up and Janet joined him. They remained that way for a moment, looking at each other in awkward silence.

"Oh, I almost forgot," Jonathon said suddenly as he reached into his pocket, pulled out a folded sheet of paper and handed it to Janet.

"What's this?" She asked as she opened it.

"It's a passage from a poem entitled Life by Charlotte Bronte. I remembered it this morning when I was packing a few books to take with me. After everything that's happened and what you've told me about Daniel, I thought it might be fitting for his bench."

Janet read the passage Jonathon had written on the paper.

"Rapidly, merrily,
Life's sunny hours flit by,
Gratefully, cheerily,
Enjoy them as they fly!"

"Yes, yes, that's perfect." Janet smiled at Jonathon and squeezed his hand. "Thank you."

"No, Janet. The thanks are all mine."

When Jonathon took a step to leave, Janet threw her arms around him, pressing her face against his chest. He wrapped one arm around her waist and stroked her hair tenderly with his other hand. They held that embrace a few minutes, and then parted. Their eyes met. Neither of them spoke. Jonathon took a few steps backward and then turned and started walking away.

After he had gone a few feet, he looked over his shoulder and called back to her, "Take care of that husband of yours. He's a good man."

Janet smiled and nodded. "I know," she whispered. "I know."

Janet watched until Jonathon and Marshall Sheffield were out of sight. Then she checked her watch. It was almost time to load their suitcases and go pick up Robert from the hospital. Scratch was going to fly them home in his Lear this afternoon. Jack Allen was picking up the tab.

Janet sighed and turned to survey the scene for the last time. The white crests of the waves rolled over the rocks as fleetingly as the intermittent clouds floated across the cerulean sky. She looked over at the lighthouse. There was no visible evidence of last week's tragic events.

The smooth stone tower of the lighthouse glistened in the bright sunshine. A pair of birds was busy making a nest in a crevice, halfway up the structure. Janet tried to peer into the windows of the watch room. It was too bright to see inside. That was probably best, Janet reflected, too many ghosts inside.

Janet lifted her gaze to the bronze seagull statue on the top of the dome. The gull was radiant in the sunlight, sitting sentinel over the cliff, with its wings rising from its body. Looking at the statue, Janet got the sense that it was on the verge of flight; ready to take off into the sky at a moment's notice to soar through the clouds.

ABOUT THE AUTHOR

Kerri Lewis is an attorney, educator, and author. After a successful law career, Kerri now dedicates her time to writing and education in her field of law. She has a BS in Business Management from Rice University and graduated with honors from the University of Texas School of Law.

Kerri lives on a small farm in Texas with her husband and dog, Sadie. She relishes the quiet beauty of her pastoral setting but appreciates lively visits from her grown children. She loves a good mystery novel and enjoys classic tales of suspense. Her debut novel Storm Surge is steeped in both genres. When she isn't working, Kerri enjoys travelling, gardening, canning, and cooking with all the fresh vegetables and herbs she grows on her farm. She's currently researching her next suspense novel, as well as a future farm project: cultivating a lavender field.